Mabel in Her Twenties

MABEL IN HER TWENTIES

*A short novel with photographs
by Rosaire Appel*

Boulder • Normal

In memory of C.R. & T.G.A.

Published by Fiction Collective Two with support given by Illinois State University, the English Department Publications Center of the University of Colorado at Boulder, the National Endowment for the Arts, and the Teachers & Writers Collaborative of New York

Address all inquiries to: Fiction Collective Two, c/o English Department, Publications Center, Illinois State University, Normal, Illinois 61761

Mabel In Her Twenties
    Rosaire Appel

ISBN: 0-932511-43-0
ISBN: 0-932511-44-9

Manufactured in the United States of America.
Distributed by the Talman Company

Typesetting and Book Design: Jean C. Lee, Carol Friedman
Cover/Jacket Design: Dave LaFleur

Though it was hers and practically her, it was not touching her person.

MABEL IN HER TWENTIES

IMMEDIATELY STRAIGHTENED the station master said once without the roar of ice, surrounded by ice and ice trains. "My travels," he argued, "have nothing beyond them though trains are apt and pretty on Sunday—waiting for me to come home." It was better to point this out than to pry, better to pry than estrange her. Or should he? Nothing about him when words had a train—most were content he suggested. To say yes or no, to smile so that one, unlike all the others, he had told her.

She wanted to leave right away.

It made no sense to go away if she could go all the way, he insisted.

"An adventure?" he offered when she sat down. The bench whose slats were peeling arranged them.

She fixed her lips and said many things over which she had said before today, a day unnaturally suited to her. A day that might be public. She would today as she was among them, looking at fate-balanced books in the distance and closing the mirror.

He frowned.

It was not as if he had told her if. "Don't you want to remember it all?" he had said. His timing and his suspicion.

"Instead of limiting, expand," he had told her.

They went a ways without crossing. Other materials developed further. History rose up from the back of her life. It was history which would be folded over—an explanation which anyone deserved—which might not be opened again.

Nobody turned out all their history, they buried history except for the seeds, a few sprigs, which they knew with good verbs. To make it both convincing and good they lived in adjustable days.

She would use what was good and amusing.

Could she have what he offered instead? She folded a fan, the train to her liking, a train for duration the station would stretch, how far could one stretch such thin tracks?

—

He came back to meet her again. Though some other woman exactly like her had turned out to be the wrong one he insisted. Young women didn't travel who weren't the right ones. She was neither the first nor the second.

She knew she could try what she liked when he faced her. She looked when he, she smiled he looked back. As if she knew who he was.

Or once or twice when she let him as if—which encouraged him as he was turning back. As he counted what she gave she turned however so slightly he thought it himself.

"With luck you'll arrive at the end," he said then. As if the end were significant.

Station masters often pointed: written directions were slow. Each track like each meal had a signal and a function. To eat in her presence, his hand to his mouth—how could one trust what was meant by the meat? One was courteous and not often candid.

"If you're hungry...?" he hinted.

They went in.

She was still not attached though slightly indebted. It was up to him to complete the next turn to ensure the leisure of her presence.

The nights were the same but thicker, when there were very few cards on the table. She had time until now she had time up till now when her future was still the future. She imagined the height and shoulders and breathing of a stranger who moved in the shadows.

"Why Hammond!" she murmured, "the station master."

Or would someone else be more desirable?

His candor was why she was courting the quick though his candor was what she wouldn't ask. His courtesy was a credential.

"Are you fatal to me?" she murmured. If others had been

they hadn't told her, how else could Mabel have had an adventure.

She didn't say what it had been, he didn't ask.

He never tried, "Where have you been?"

If he had only courtesy to his credit, she had no intention of falling. Though they took separate courses each one came back, each one expecting an offer. This one held firm: it was tender. This one held firm: it was useful.

Some things could be useful for her and her father. Who else would encourage the useful? A father who had little left over. He had a car for future occasions and he always had something to swallow, which he swallowed. If Mabel would also have something to swallow, she would mind she must mind what was righteous to take.

She made some arrangements for taking.

Coming and going as if she'd stopped praying—no one should have to be coaxed.

Hammond coaxed a little and stopped. Most people deserve some proof, she argued. She was willing to share some amusement as proof she was yielding so far she could even be tender. She expanded him and. She studied him and. She reviewed the face that he left behind—it was natural with a little desperation.

This one agreed that the future was blank, that one had had something to hide. Could only a father find fault?

Her father was a feather behind her.

She sometimes liked to tell people this, they could use it when they thought of her. No thought could grasp the killing of birds, but for one in that way, for amusement.

Mabel had plenty of amusement and clothing. Those who had neither had little acceptance. She sometimes, she sometimes had somewhat less. What she would if she could: a clean slate.

"You must seek to please Him," her father had told her equating himself at each fork in the road.

Mabel had rolled down the window.

It happened that she had plenty to amuse her, the sun was shining on men in the meadows. Her past had its back to the light. Whatever she passed the details new outlines and over it all was a blanket. A picnic blanket and a basket. She smiled. A blanket was a furnishing for the future her future when she would have many picnics.

She would say, "Some have picnics on tables with chairs." And Hammond would rise and oil the hinges. He would ease and agree to be eased, she would bet.

Chairs kept catching her eye.

If she wanted to have them with him—would he ask? Or would be cautious and stall.

Would he stall and then would he true?

With a difficult sidelong pitch he attempted to sidetrack her quest for a perfect picnic. He worked for his life for his own revision, and not many had swayed him though here she was smiling and laying her glove on his sleeve.

She was driving her father's new car.

Last summer he'd walked without anyone else although he had not been alone. There had been others in that town that summer of days he had come to by train.

That summer with trains at the end of each train at the end of each evening no effort to meet them. Trains and few picnics between.

Many people needed trains in those days.

Many also needed a father and some needed feathers and others had flowers. If flowers were facing the neighbor's parlor one cut them slyly or cut not at all. Even the ones that were weeds. If one had reason to want them and keep them, though dying they looked pretty and good. Even in a meadow one lingered longer, even in a meadow one injured more slowly.

Hammond was apparently uninjured. He was by his means and effective. He knew how to kiss, he knew to push, to get through the thick and the thin and get back. Not all were able to accomplish a friction that everyone felt was thrilling. Condensation at that instant was expected. Some people especially those starting out were apt to be more experimental.

But though trains disappeared they returned.

He went up to her she had everything else, she had distance even at a distance and tulips.

"How many trains left?" she asked everyone else as though there were none in the station. As though she preferred empty tracks.

There would be but for now there were not. When the space was reduced the picture was this: a pulpit, a cake supporting white icing set hard as cement with nobody sinking. The right surface had to be set. The bed was smooth and aligned. The person Mabel was meant to be would rise up by the man both tall and withstanding. He would give what he'd had by himself which was separate and never with anyone else. Once she had risen and changed her name she wouldn't mind walking at all, she believed. She'd agree to leave things behind. Yet if she became what they clearly opposed—what would they offer her then?

Hammond waited in a park. He did not wear gloves nor did she. There were others accompanying Hammond and Mabel as long as they longed to keep going correctly. As long as they laughed and kept moving. No one brought blankets nor traveled to hide, they didn't hide and seek, they looked calm. Their calmness made them seem neutral. Trees were clever and hills were imported, the paths for the sake of advancing and passing depending on customs and matter. Depending on tulips and chatter. Thus Hammond and Mabel echoed each other— he pointed she whispered each tried to give pleasure. He pointed she tried not to seem very eager.

Yet if someone else was writing a name and a time for Mabel to settle in better, if—and how would she know? She said this she said she might settle for Hammond. She said she and Hammond might go.

It was a three-quarter laugh he issued, published then censored, one laugh then another. Did it fall on the side of the side of derision?

He glanced at the world.

She saw his lapel.

There were millions of similar sightings among them. He was starting to realize she knew where she was and where she had been with others. Which absolved him. He didn't read the names on her sleeve. If this was symbolic, the names on her sleeve, the brim of his hat, it was also agreed.

"It's like a tulip," he said to her, warming the side of her face that looked cold.

Turning she said, "Are you cold?" He stopped grinning.

11

They went up and they faced side by side.
Hammond was fond of where he was pleased and when he was leading he favored each part. He had volumes of parts he had squeezed. Long before Mabel had slender excuses, for telling her finally some things she should read. "But Hammond I already know!" she argued. Just as she and just like the ones she herself had often been treated, she told him. As she took Hammond's hand he did nothing to counter the date and the purpose—ignored them.
"What would you do in my favor?" she asked.
For a man who received he would never give in, he arrived at Mabel's with boasting. It wasn't much more than the place where she lived, nor was it a place he could go to for nothing. The fair all around and accusing. A union, an offering, an opinion: accusing.
"What would you do in my favor?" she asked him looking to see him without her. She had moved somewhat closer than he. Some moves had been carefully made while others on Sunday in particular had been careless. When Hammond's arms were heavily folded she could not be certain because he did nothing. She was, because he did nothing untoward, those scenes with flattering lines forgotten. He'd said them in just the right tone.
Love is like a tulip, thought Mabel, and tulips should not be uprooted.
He had never not taken her hand.
He had always agreed where it counted.
Thus with Hammond Mabel might tie, the right tie, a knot with a future everlasting.
If he asked would she be so inclined?
This was basic: she would be as if the nights were all the same length but thicker. This was true with few cards on the table for Mabel had had only future quick scenes.
On her way home she had had them.
In the car with the window rolled down she had more.
Most knew those quick scenes, private cars. Most knew what they knew without turning around to see what was happening behind them. She said she knew what they knew. For they echoed her laughter with definite weight that started from who had been kissing, they told her.

MABEL IN HER TWENTIES

No one would want second place.

Pleading would satisfy any public if he made Mabel an offer, she thought.

But he sometimes lost track of the trains he dispatched and the tons and the tours that followed. This was how Hammond was. He had plenty of tours to choose from now and he wasn't unhappy that he could go freely. He might down a beer before going. He might dream up a sequel because of it.

Yet saw her and was not the same.

Here there were lips to light or to lean, he eyed her as he tried moving over. When he tried to place the lips right, however, he had to conclude he was with her.

She was standing beside a piano.

"Do you play?" she asked.

He pushed back his sleeves.

She saw him digress the next second.

But Hammond didn't see himself digressing didn't see himself playing, she winked he winked back. She smiled which many people did in a way that was suitably charming.

Allowing the smile he said that her smile was bowed and beautifully pending.

"Pending," Mabel repeated.

She began to think that his playing was practical and he kept nothing but records.

Sometimes the book on her lap fell closed, other times they played cards they drove cars. Some never sat at a window because of it simply looking out of a window.

—

Instead, Mabel's father was looking out the window, surely ready if Hammond should come. Mabel also was ready surely. Conclusions in those days were left to the father, if Hammond offered to be this man's son. It was he who would have to carry the family because it was always a family sons carried.

Feathers. A steeple. Blue sky.

She left the book open on her lap to a bird, a falcon torn through the middle. The background was better than most it was clean.

"Look!" Hammond noticed, "an eagle!"
This brought him back into the game with Mabel who broke her first promise which ended her past. She held up her name, as if nothing undoing, as if she were merely going upstairs. She went up. As if she were only going up to come down, she went up and then she came down. She was agreeable when they were together. And as changeable as charts on the back of a chair. It was actually part of the bargain. Flirtation should be contagious. They would have plenty of time on the threshold, his presence and hers, refunding all others.

Even his presence could still be refunded and hers in a message that was fashionable was encouraging.

A week passed.

Although there were other young men in the wings who whistled it could only be Hammond she heard. It was Hammond. To a scene which replayed itself on its own she added simple variations. All her scenes had this at least: enough tension for a definite beginning.

Hammond had some of his own for himself for a promise had not yet been stated. Though a few said that marriage was continually rewarding, most of them left this unsaid.

If not for reward, why be attached?

Mabel had won the first round.

"And if I meet your father?" he asked.

Mabel knew his words and said nothing. A woman must take some things with her in silence. Thus Hammond didn't see her gathering in silence, and she was well-suited and often.

And he liked having a definite often. It was making and giving him more in her favor—though changing and fixing his comings and goings.

They could never be introduced now.

Yet when he was somewhere else was she also? Or was she counting their common efforts, waiting for him to say where they were? If he had come with no destination he hadn't been whistling at all, he asserted.

When she gave him a pen he asked her again, "Did you think I was somebody else?"

Few people had patience for that.

What was best was often occasional for Mabel who refused to quit or go back. "Perhaps someone else," she admitted.

It would seem as they spoke he had traveled she listened: he told her he traveled at very great speeds in his quest to get to the end.

Mabel looked behind him again. It was true he was often in a rush. It was true he was better with intimate pleasure when no verbal passages linked them together. Still words had been cut and spliced together some sentences forcibly filled to the end. Mabel sat down on the bench.

No one liked an empty feeling yet no one liked feeling too full. Her future was not yet full in fact it was leaking and anyone who was anyone could see it. Private courts and no second opinion either, they were playing in opposite directions.

Hammond didn't see what she meant.

When he didn't know what she meant, what rules ruled, when he didn't know the point he slowed down. Each minute took longer than a minute.

Irrelevance could be occasionally accepted if there were guests to distract him.

Was Mabel still possibly a stranger?

She laughed. "My name is Mabel," she told him. She had always wanted to be perfect.

He didn't see the only possible point: that this was the way she was on Wednesday. He wondered what else was acceptable.

Yet it thrilled him sometimes to take turns. They took turns. This brought them back to the square where they'd met, they'd been here before, no promise, no conclusion. Mabel was still very young. She said it was true she was young and that he, that all he had known was approval.

He heard what she said and said no.

"It's just a formality," she hedged.

Was she this way because of her family? he wondered. This led him back—she was fond of pretending—Mabel was telling him something to prove she was always like this she insisted.

Or was it because he was flattering?

He had no way of knowing at whom and for what was she crying when she cried like this. He wasn't supposed to be wrong.

When Hammond did not know what he was causing he changed the subject or put on a record.
Mabel sometimes knew what he meant.

—

Though it wasn't a question Mabel said she was actually doing very well at the moment. If indeed they all were they would measure her strictly to find out exactly how well. Which they did.
But Mabel refused to tell.
Primary facts were what they wanted, they said they'd been raised to expect nothing less. They intended eventually to have their own memoirs and Mabel might be included.
But Mabel was threading her needle.
This exchange was a custom among people so frequently no one considered it.
After questioning her they went back to themselves. They couldn't tell where she was headed. Thus Mabel might leave them behind or they her. They slipped back to where they belonged. She had made a choice it seemed to them, as they slipped further away.
They weren't slipping however but retreating.
Or Mabel appeared to be retreating from every proposal, from justification. Anything useful was justification, the rest could be swept off the table.
She was sweeping in several directions.

—

Then when he had next to nothing remaining, Hammond decided he liked Mabel's laugh. He folded his maps which encouraged her. As if they had come to the middle and paused, she could never know too much about him he thought.
Because of this he stayed upright.
Being upright made him seem useful.
He found Mabel easily adding more reasons, daily, to most of his habits. What habits? Leaving the cost in the margins. If he were bitter if he were lazy—as if he had sometimes known love

that was better. Nor would he ever if he would agree with no one but Mabel beside him.

Many agreed without divulging that they were not always agreeable. Thus each year some lovers were left over. Many wore similar hats. Many felt similar hates. Still the population kept growing.

If sometimes it seemed to mean nothing else, it made at least a curious collection—a population that continued affecting the planet on which they were breeding. Who knew what else it could come to mean unless they sometimes gave in together?

They gave in to what couldn't be said.

Some women gave in with proof of reasons, some men with reason appealed. Many still wanted to discover something that many still said didn't exist. They hurried along to the end to discover if proof were actually in the beginning and what was being hidden in the middle.

Since the end was the point to Hammond he hurried.

She kissed him taking her time with his cheek.

When his cheek was held by lips upon it, he could not hurry yet he had to give in.

"May I give in?" Hammond asked. "May I give in yet?" he pleaded.

"What snowdrifts," she said in a voice lacking passion. Nothing at all had happened.

There was hope in his voice in the second round. "Are you pretending?" he wanted to know, though he was not fond of asking.

He rose abruptly took off his jacket to sit by her side and admire the tulips. She was only turning the pages, absorbed— she was only turning some pages. She was not by his side in the least. She told him that summer was over.

It was autumn.

If she became engaged to him she would give him the rest of her time she told him, and he in turn would have to give his except when he was working.

Hammond said quite a bit less.

This was the first step put forth by a daughter whose father insisted she finish her life. That is she should finish what he had started, make smooth what he had left rough.

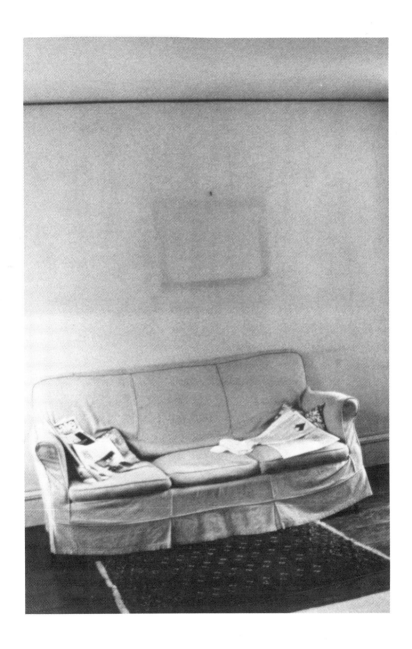

If she didn't try she should vanish.

For failure, there was no excuse. Few were permitted to have an excuse: failure was failure was fault.

Yet if no one knew Mabel or Mabel's father how could he or she find fault? If she should go where she pleased.

What Mabel couldn't carry she'd leave.

What Mabel couldn't have she would borrow.

The most she would fear getting caught in between, if she went where she was seen.

She began to find it amusing. A fate that no one else had courted, she smiled to herself, Suppose I get caught? They sang standing up close together. No one dared leave until everyone finished thus everyone stayed to the end.

Mabel was leaving that night.

If somebody near her, a clerk who didn't count, would be handsome in time, he was young. She didn't dare address him directly however she asked a question without direction. She sometimes did this sometimes not.

"When's the next train?" she addressed the room.

She thought, "Should I carry a cane?"

He was hidden in himself unobserved. He was nearly as important as inconsequential, she would not ask him about blankets on the train. Nobody wished in a well. Mabel left very quickly that evening the details of it and a night on the train.

She who had been moving since birth with details still confined to a dream—sometimes she stood to one side of the middle without looking back without looking forward and could not say where she had been.

One side was turned upside down.

The other had little distinction until she discovered that something was missing.

She decided that nothing was missing.

If Hammond would finish what he'd started she concluded, nothing at all would be missing.

"Hammond," she said, "has five brothers." She didn't know their names or the names of their wives but she didn't think not-knowing should stop her from going.

She bought a book about sons, he didn't stop her. All women are interested in sons he asserted. A son was the one who would have the last straw—and all women because of it were proper. Then Hammond carried Mabel's luggage through streets with sufficient history to them. She saw at a glance because they were there as if they belonged in that position, as if there were nothing in the world but this.

"Might there be something else?" he teased.

Two things about warmth and a rhythmic motion which often made young men smile.

Poor Mabel skipped over the rest.

"All my life," Hammond said trying to have his own way, "trains were a few minutes late."

When he spoke again he was contrite. "A few minutes here or there is nothing."

She forgave him, she was still very young.

Together they missed the next train completely but at Christmas she went back to her father.

—

The mind of a father was lasting, everlasting. And any mistake was not his. For him it was fate if there was blame. Yet Mabel implied he was wrong.

There was hope was it hope or hunger within her? For the first time she studied his clothing. She withdrew her arms from those sleeves.

"I will tell you the history of men," he told her.

"Which men?"

It would be a surprise.

Though Mabel had always liked surprises, at dinner she decided to marry Hammond. The clever got richer her mother had taught her—fortuitous details, the rest seen half-blind. Her mother could always tell one from the other the rich from the wrong the wise from the blind, although men looked mostly the same.

Now Mabel's sister suspected something and though Mabel was silent she continued developing certain themes they had sworn to conceal. Had she paid her sister to hate her? They paid each had paid and unkind.

Thus her sister willfully revealed the fact that Mabel had met just the man, a just man, whose picture she already had as proof. Madeline herself had seen it. A picture of him at war.

"He isn't part of the war," Mabel countered, offering him now as he was. She would change any question of tact with tact, thus Mabel said nothing against Madeline for telling. She wouldn't tell the difference between them now, what she kept to herself for later.

"Shall I describe him?" Madeline persisted.

"If it is Hammond I already know," said Mabel because they were sisters.

Poor Hammond she thought of the future briefly his trains and his training and breathing.

Some months would pass that could also be seasons for those who did what they pleased. Which is to say that some couldn't. It was short too short without pausing for some while others were now in training.

They had time and now time had run out.

—

Whatever she wanted to obtain whatever she wanted she looked at their lips. Plenty of lips were new. There were lips while most of the others had dinner each night at twilight that Mabel was sensing. Her own lips however were sealed. She would not reveal each wish each rule each time she tried to afford what was new. Sometimes one tried and one paid.

A man who paid and a woman kept roving that they could still explain. He should have enough proof to explain. He must be willing to spend the proof on her, a desirable substance with no strings attached unless they were kept out of sight. Marionette strings, that invisible. If this required specific occasions low voices the money concealed in the binding. Could anyone come to be trusted? Could Hammond have, and now could Harmon?

Harmon was the one who would whisper. No one should slide a glance toward the binding he kept it concealed by his plate. He continued talking as if addition were only the way people were, where they went. This was the way that some started. They had noticed each other as soon as they entered and like others had been encouraged to do so. At least she assumed that this way was reserved for her when Harmon entered.

When Mabel's shoes pinched they belonged to her sister, it was part of the listening to learn this. She was saying almost as much as her sister, saying perhaps all evening she said it as if with no other intention. Mabel knew Harmon was surprised. She saw he was also impatient. A single Mabel had sat down at the table, a single Mabel and her sister. If this were known as she went in: he didn't live among tables and chairs. He lived among white open spaces.

When Harmon asked what he thought she was thinking— himself his own body his open division—his money neither negated nor proved it though given the best explanation. "Adorable," he whispered, "sweet." She went in when he left it ajar.

Through a look at the dresser to pictures uncovered, she thought it was strange nothing happened completely. He had many more pictures than naming. "Your wish is my instruction," he whispered, his favorite recording and led her to standing. She looked at the place he had won, he was kneeling. It never failed to move him deeply in that way with Mabel standing before him. The moment closed with his pulse pounding. He stroked her arm he was lost beside her, as if caught they moved even closer and clung.

At least that was what she imagined.

He had offered no extension however and should not be trusted by rote. To assume an extension by rote in passing— she'd been taught what would fail and to whose reputation. Some men would have even less patience, he warned, he disposed of her pretty-faced pleas right away. She wouldn't want anyone's pretty-faced man, "Would you?" he demanded.

"Whatever you say," she complied.

"Whatever I say?" he persisted.

Mabel said maybe she would try. Playing the two and a deeper arrangement, with echoes from each, not all of them sanguine, not all of them on every page. The longer the echo their elbows and tulips, which was said by her eyes in one look.

Harmon didn't read all looks however for some men wavered where other men cheated.

What he missed was the echo of listening.

Later Harmon might have little left when he reached in his pocket took out his felt cap, alone in the tunnel without her. He must be patient with rhymes he decided and her name and the rhythm and the heat.

"Just for now," she had said before leaving.

The pride and the plain of Harmon's face when he asked her what would come next, she was leaving: this was her alternate track. Anyone could try to stay where she promised—anyone who drank to reach and crossed over—try harder, one had, to pick oneself up or else one gave in to the vague.

—

Mabel each time was glad to give in, the close call the hall closed and its paper. The glass was empty, the table clean, her voice alone guarding the echo within her.

When Mabel looked up set saw Hammond. The table before her was already set, she could never go back nor erase his small lies. If she had to have this and be married, she thought—she would take getting married in hand.

"Your sister will be happily married," some prompted.

"If she is someone, someone will chose her."

They smiled as she said it and told her. Hammond had sat by her sister, they told her. Hammond had sat with her cousin.

And Hammond himself had known a few things, that weekend because the transom was open. He had had some unusual dreams. He had caught himself glaring and sweating in the morning when he was usually inert.

Now he left Mabel and her sister and her cousin to become the nearly erased. To have Mabel who filled him with questions, he told her, by her alone could he be found. He would be wherever she found him, he told her. He promised that he could be found.

Mabel remained at home.

The sun was bright the home was intact. Mabel moved as if she were drowning. She must get rid of the water, she thought, those who stayed in it were certain of drowning.

Did anyone wish to go out?

She had nearly forgotten what she had hoped for. Her posture because of him and reclining.

To stretch this reclining—perfection was formidable—performance foretelling some splendid occasion, a dress would have to be made. A veil would have to be worn and then lifted by hands that were not her own. It is better to give than be rested she thought, better to give in than be wrested. If she thought he would want her to stay and she would, it was this, it would be Hammond not Harmon.

Though she was pale she must be generous while everyone else was taking her time. Picking tulips and taking her time. If someone wanted to tell her something she stopped and went forth where he or she wanted. Why couldn't she go where she pleased?

It was this she thought as she tied and was tying. It was not something said to him now she concluded, still willing to try it completely. Trying not to tie it too loosely either as the groom and his family would put on their hats, their requisite hats for the service. They didn't ask they didn't have to ask where to sit. They looked to the bride for justification and sat on the opposite side.

A bride had exactly one minute more rope. The bride even now—others strolled by the trees. There would not be more confirmation than this, but for pride the stock phrases compatible with cake. It took less to spoil a future than this, both Mabel and Madeline as women were reminded.

Have you had enough cake? they were asked to ask. Have you had enough fate? Were you forced to surrender?

They might have asked Harmon also. He had the same answers as everyone else, even if one slipped up in the asking.

Mabel had mattered no asking.

"You shall always have Hammond instead!" Harmon told her pretending to give her more rope.

"I'm going to have to pay for that for the rest of my life?" she demanded.

With another to pay for the rest of one's life it made one uncomfortable taking sometimes.

If it were hot they would not rehearse, if their house was wherever they wanted to have it. But a father could be disagree-

able. He spoke to them of the cellar, the store room—which he shouldn't have had to mention at all.

"Foundations must be exact," said her father from one to the other one evening.

For Mabel still had her father and her mother. And if she'd had nothing in the other direction her father and mother would not contradict her, side by side with the bride as their cake. Mabel's mother and father with their hands on a cake that Mabel was trying to take from them.

They pulled.

She added and subtracted enough to remind them of what they had had and what they had wanted. She did this in lines that were watered, which bled. Therefore each one seemed different. She even used words that crossed out the fact that her father had often annoyed her.

She had memorized each sentence each fact.

"I'm changing my likes and dislikes," she told Harmon one day in the midst of her memorization.

He himself had a much lighter touch that was soothing. She was better she told him because she was soothed—with iced tea and somewhere to sit. It was her own and well-lighted prediction—once she had learned what her father had said. His likes and dislikes were not hers.

Each moment extended the outcome then, an outcome that was three times as private as money was quick and attention scattered. In this way they extended their moments.

A man who was stunning was usually intended and the right shadow accompanied each feature. And someone less stunning—an ace in the grass in the garden some said it had happened to Mabel. She had put her hand into the lake, they said, she had put a smooth stone to her lips. She had seized others and she had been taken and made so in her own voice, they said.

But her voice was usually amusing now she was gathering reflections for Harmon. She was giving her father cut flowers. This was the duty of daughters to fathers: to give them no cause to curse them. If he refused she should not accuse him and if he completely she made herself gray.

Mabel went in to her father.

He said to her, "What will you ask?" This was where he had

always been living near his fireplace and his convictions.
How able is Harmon he would ask.
    She made herself tell him with proper revision for someone
like him who was overly cautious. He never rehearsed with
either daughter which made his sentences considerably longer.
He refused to be hurried by either daughter standing apart from
their father.

—

While Mabel unaccountably knew Harmon by choice,
through the noise the pulse of a Hammond remembered—the
actual Hammond stepped onto the platform, the actual
Hammond approached. Remembering forgotten details about
him Mabel saw Hammond return.
    The way he sat still in the car. He sat in the car as he if he
would always sit in that car without moving. Among friends he
thought he should smile. He would choose the right subjects for
Mabel with pleasure and Mabel would know him because of it.
    Some trains and scenery were required.
    Nor could Mabel ignore Hammond now as he paused on the
threshold and entered their parlor. He was tepid with accounts
of himself.
    Yet he still had the right to himself.
    He shook out his cuffs as if someone were watching. All
through the meal he thought someone was watching. Cuffs were
still required as were creases, shoelaces and ties for each dinner.
    Now Hammond had an honorable expression. When hands
were extended how warm he exuded the moment for Mabel's
concern.
    Mabel stared at the floor even more.
    He knew he shouldn't say what he felt as she stared, her
attention restricted to the floor.
    A reach though within easy reach he should not, nor take the
last piece overlapping. Yet once his preference had been accepted it seemed to Hammond who often listened, he was
listening to water running.
    Two shades of grey appeared in the morning. Each one
reflected in a mirror. She would take one gray for herself she

decided while the others were still at the breakfast table. She believed that she hoped they would stay. She would tell them that Hammond had made some arrangements, or she would laugh as if to detain them. Then she would become an original person who had started out being only Mabel.

There was not much commotion on the street.

There is not much commotion he was thinking while waiting for Mabel to come around. Nor was there much in the past he guessed as he gathered more of the same. He had no compunction against gathering sentences to spread throughout anyone's day.

"I've met someone else," he heard Mabel saying in contrast to what he'd been thinking of saying.

"Let's see him!"

"Don't you believe me?"

He yawned he was falling asleep. He fell this way as he fell every night, some instinct knew not to protest.

No method no purpose unwound to amuse him as Hammond was counting dogs as he slept. Even as he protested they barked and he was completely asleep. It was nothing for many not matched. In the back of his dreams it could easily happen, he didn't have the time light them completely, didn't have to have all her concern.

In a dream nothing happened to counter it.

Hammond gave into deep sleeps. Moving along he followed the details were tangled he pulled himself up. The transom was open and someone was laughing. He went to the door and looked out. Did she notice him hiding like that?

She had been saying the same thing all summer: he didn't see the point of finality. He had squeezed himself into their midst once again for Mabel who would always be Mabel. But when someone was visiting everyone looked and everyone wanted to see where he went. He went in and sat down, had iced tea with lemon.

Mabel stayed in her room.

There were fields of corn near the lake there were cousins. Mabel mostly stayed in her room. She had seen his hands his arms to the elbow but not all at once as she now he was naked. Beside her in bed and then he was gone.

She had seen his shadows uncreased. Later when Mabel sat down to lunch he spoke as he should, as if she, and stayed on. Yet she said to him earlier than ever that evening, "Goodnight." This time his portrait absorbed it. "It was I who stepped into the house," he reminded. "Obviously!" Mabel retorted. Hammond strode out of the parlor. The frame around the picture was wrong, the picture was wrong, the wrong was wrong. It was Sunday already and Hammond was leaving and Mabel was still in her room.

Hammond was held in the pit of his longing, he wasn't himself but pulled down by his longing. He realized that frames were not mere decoration, they were practical devices of preservation. Even the door ahead was a frame, even sleep, even kissing and trains. The yard the steps through some very pause— an advantage could change in the flick of a pause.

Now Hammond had no indication. He had never stayed in that pause between pleasure like everyone else for so long. He was already beginning to tell it to seal it for himself with her outside his court. She had interest and often again and he knew it, she was moving forward and everyone saw her. Though his presence lingered on several occasions, he was tall and had never been quaint.

He didn't cough to get her attention.

His initials his examples unfinished unhooked were no use in a crisscrossed convention. Sometimes a man won and then vanished.

Hammond said he might tour the planet but that would not mean he had vanished.

If he had indigestion he blamed the restaurant, he blamed the mattress, blamed the heat. Still he swore that he could not vanish.

He had a narrow file perhaps a table a definite bed. A chart and a chair, a chair chart. He used these to prop up his plan. Every man wanted to have a plan, like his father before him caught in the same glove.

A plan that would make him complete.

Even Mabel sometimes caught sight of a plan, if it looked like a glove, she tried it on. Mabel that is who had followed him back, the Mabel who now looked over his shoulder. She hardly heard what he thought however she would only hear what was promised. This would be the heart of the matter much later when Hammond went back to the war.

—

When Mabel and Hammond were evenly parted with considerable interest invested between them. Each had a significant plan. Although there were movies to guide them through it, speed in the movies no caution, much glass.

He had hardly heard Mabel much better.

"How I miss you!" he usually and Mabel began. He usually and Mabel agreeable. The sunsets were also agreeable lately as flowers were, that is they were liked by those who were not allergic.

"What will you have?" someone asked her.

She said, "I might and I might not."

She would not be responsible for anything whispered, the extra effort of meeting their eyes, the extra effort of constant attention while Mabel was thinking of Hammond.

She sorted her desirable dresses. For the young in their own were more easily selected, Mabel as well as her sister mattered. Their latent questions, she warded them off, exchanged them for hasty exemptions.

If they told her she wore the wrong hat she borrowed her sister's and that was that. Her mother, standing behind her by habit, had nothing more suitable to offer.

One day she had a note from Hammond's mother and the next day she kindly replied.

For Hammond had his mother behind him. She had polished his shoes with her own every morning, arranged her own and impeccable choosing as she went from one side to the other. Her days had four sides and five meals at least. Her days were displayed with a lack of despair that was visible to anyone coming or going. Only the nights were erratic. Only their pauses,

a lack of provision. But when people in daylight were standing with Hammond, his mother was often beside him.

Mabel was not yet among them except in name they were given her name.

He had had a full lunch with her father.

Although he had little else in common with her more erratic immediacy tried, he'd gone up to Mabel's reflection and waited. His mother had fused with the wallpaper behind him.

The arrangement of what exactly happened could never be kept in reflections however. This too was how countries behaved. They had similar eyes which they shut. Their digressions and ornaments reflected each other—how one behaved, if one looked like the rest, everyone thought this was best.

Some doors would be opened some wouldn't.

The windows were closed it was autumn.

Though many kept on with a definite weight with a definite future around them each evening, each morning brought more of the same.

There was something to be said for more of the same if the rest did not sink just to rise. If it stayed sunk where it was. If it fused with what was under. At the end others mused on what rose and what sank, white roses and red ones on top. There would always be others who tried to shift meanings and others who simply gave up. A few things that happened would be recorded, a marriage, a banquet, a single torn eagle. And some things that were given would be kept.

Now Mabel had been where she'd been. Her primary goal had failed at least twice and now she took trains whenever she found them.

Mabel wanted only to be happy.

She still had some hopes that could make her seem better to give to be good, and she also received. She expected all this as well. Sometimes her mother and sometimes her father—but the details didn't always reach them. He owned the alley he owned Mabel's sister—that was enough of a plot for Mabel. He'd had time and things that had taken time that were finished and polished while Mabel had not.

Mabel only wanted to be happy.

It took all her time for her share of the best taking turns

coming into a room. In the presence of others and while one was speaking, neither whispering nor weeping, as if one were best. In this way one kept oneself light. In this way one made oneself durable.

Even Mabel was durable.

She thought of Hammond in her father's presence, and Hammond in the room so brutally uncovered. She outlined her own performance then and studied the palm of her hand. There were primary goals and demands. There were primary coals and diamonds. Only a diamond a groom a house of her own and weather permitting.

She imagined him closer already. She imagined Hammond whenever she could she was already drawing designs without doubt for the future, her future, to claim. He would come and the future would obey.

Or the future would come and he would obey.

He would take the place of her own ever after—in this way Mabel was expecting Mabel to become like everyone else.

When Christmas was over and the others well-fixed, Mabel began to buy what she needed. In the light it was pretty, in that light. Mabel felt she had something to go on. A mirror had nothing more to tell her she told her mother those thoughts which would please her.

But her mother instructed her sister instead. "One day your husband will come," she told her. For Madeline was surely tied to that place and Mabel was asking for trouble.

It was the custom of that place at that time that those without ties were cut off. Thus the custom was to keep busy tying for anything tied could be useful. This kept many going, which was useful. To stop was to matter with everything else, to stop was to say one had failed.

Now Harmon asked Madeline about her sister whenever he saw her, he used his own words. He went directly to the subject as even Madeline would not. She had seen others take a full subject that way without anything touching. She knew in a daydream she knew what was happening when Harmon asked for her sister.

Madeline herself was richer than many and twice as effective with talented courage. She tore off her hat when she laughed. If time they still had was repeated in common she was looking at Harmon she knew him by heart.

The windows were small the wind blowing. "Harmon!" cried Mabel as if she had lost him. She wasn't listless could now interrupt, she knew how the third person mattered.

The stories Madeline and Mabel could tell! The voices and fortunes of others they'd touched, to be drawn to be quartered and not without boasting.

Harmon however no longer needed to ask what he openly asked. He knew. Her reply was only politeness to him, an answer sewn into the middle.

Or had Mabel left him forever?

He didn't have much of a father for instance his father was his own but had never belonged. Mabel knew this he reflected. She was often touched by his effort his postcards she often touched his sleeve freely and held it. And only she and then Madeline that summer, as only Mabel at the end had won out. But Mabel had been there with others before him repeating each sentence that summer.

Still neither Mabel nor Madeline had given anything that they could not take back. They were sisters when they were together.

One couldn't see Mabel without Madeline that summer, couldn't see her without different spacing. And each was considering the other's spacing, each wanted to be much too pretty. To have what she wanted at the heart of the family, neither Mabel nor Madeline were idle.

Nothing good happened when one was idle.

No one should idle in daylight.

Nor should one idle in winter while the father was hauling wood for the fire.

Anyone else could carry wood who was young and not idle nor dreaming he told them. What he couldn't carry he left. His daughters stayed in and kept warm. An outlined arm, a basket of knitting—the sisters sat on the couch.

Mabel and Madeline were sisters together especially when they were knitting.

—

One day Hammond walked up the block. His hair was smooth his eyes identical for the sisters sitting on the porch. Their sitting would partially unsettle him. To take what he offered as long as they stayed within sight of each other he was asking. They went inside they were laughing.

But Madeline immediately met someone else and Mabel was left with time on her hands, her own time, her own hands, Mabel studied her hands. Then she studied the impact of Hammond's hand he had left an impression of them in her mind. Other times she was less ambitious. She never offered any explanation.

Then Madeline initially had more than Mabel, was flashing a ring whose radiance confirmed she was already better because of it. She knew who she was going to be: instead of sitting, carrying. Serving instead of consuming. Anyone could see how the hands were set how the time was set like a watch that had stopped on a wrist still warm and moving.

Madeline had announced she was ready.

Then Madeline was taught how to breathe in his presence was taught when to stop and start in his presence. She learned that a little more than once would ruin him or would gradually secure him. She would learn to fill the empty up and to empty what was full. She had to prevent overreaching from either must always arrive as if he were successful.

"His name is Hugo," she told them.

"Disaster can change a perspective," they warned her, failure followed by failure and so on, even because of a war. Other subjects would not be available during the process of failure, they warned her.

"What does he like?" Mabel asked her.

Mabel still holding Hammond's hand, had no way of knowing who she was holding or was she making him up? Even on the threshold within her she dreamed that she might be making him up. Mabel could deliberately try it.

Meanwhile nothing noticeable happened. She walked beside Harmon and stood beside Harmon and throughout the city there were plenty of Harmons. Mabel didn't know what they wanted.

She sometimes stayed in her room.

But Mabel could no longer live without a favorable opinion concealed in a passion. To fluctuate nicely between them behind them even if they were standing apart.

Was she waiting for Hammond to find her?

He was waiting for guests at the track. Plenty of men who meant nothing else, would do the same thing while they hummed the same tune. Their goal was the object of monotony.

Then Mabel began to be glad. Because she knew nothing about Hammond now, she pictured how they would go up together. She would go up as she pleased.

She would go up the same way every time, it was best to know how to expect to go up, now that she expected to be going. She laughed. "I am waiting," she said to Harmon, "for Hammond. Just as you predicted."

Not everything mattered at that distance.

If she kissed him and went out for instance, if not and not always the same. She must not always be the same she knew she was destined to despise him again.

She studied the ashtray and thought of herself, looked again at the door that would open tomorrow or the next day when Hammond came back.

Mabel meanwhile could laugh softly. "I'm about to cave in in every direction!" She told them while she was waiting. It was merely a line to be mentioned.

"I really am caving in!" she exclaimed.

"Shall we go out?" Harmon interrupted.

Before Mabel answered he told her again what he had begun to suspect. It was this: there was nothing endearing left over. His own name when she said it was full of derision thus Harmon wanted to stop.

"How particular you are!" Mabel told him.

Could one unparticular have passed? Acceptable embellishments though usually slight still had to have roots in extremes. If he had not been extreme all along it was not as if he could be now.

Mabel did better than that. She wasn't concealing that she was looking and waiting to take the best seat.

"How particular!" she said again laughing.

They went back and exchanged what could be exchanged they went back to where they could take turns. When anyone said I have something to offer she looked at the line that was there for the taking.

"I like to see pictures," she said.

Poor Harmon had nothing to show. No one bothered him, no one knew him as nearly as he knew anyone else. This kindled a certain passion within him though laughing too little was habitual.

Neither Mabel nor Harmon nor anyone near them was drenched in excessive delight.

The part they came to was familiar this time as they came to some benches and trees.

"Do you remember?" he asked her.

"Mabel would you like to remember?" he pleaded.

Mabel took out her mirror.

So much depended on gaining control of the light in midwinter, that kind of light, reluctant to be how one wanted.

She was a woman who wanted to be Mabel. Yet a portion of Mabel was everyone else who was trying for more interesting facts.

"I've told you some interesting facts," she contended. Harmon was holding his head in his hands.

"Are you sure there will be someone else?" he murmured.

Mabel was both reassuring and destined. She only said what she wanted to say. If she in time would doubt this approach, that time had not yet arrived.

Then she turned and noticed their progress. They had eaten as much as everyone else, and intended to have something more. Talking was just one more duty they practiced as they were sitting and eating together.

They were being together enough, he insisted.

This wasn't for Mabel the proof that she needed, she needed everything else.

"Proof of what?" Harmon asked.

"Of the future."

He laughed. "Where will you meet someone else?"

"On Wednesday at seven," she replied.

How could Mabel be certain? She was gradually certain of quite a bit less and he turned to reminded her and Mabel fell silent. They sat in silence undisturbed by the silence that concealed everything else.

Now Mabel knew that she lacked ways of knowing and sometimes she had to pretend what she knew. Too far in the present she'd left much behind and the future was often opaque.

"Proof of what?" Harmon asked her again. He said she was making the wrong decision to exclude him to remove him—he took up the slack.

Mabel disputed very little.

"Madeline," he said, "has said more."

"Perhaps she has but she's still after all, Madeline is still my sister."

Harmon's locution grew strained. Harmon between today and tomorrow would find something else he would want but couldn't touch. He hadn't touched Mabel which was permissible—after which Mabel had had quite enough.

Yet Harmon was still optimistic.

Mabel felt pure and essential.

He envied the privilege of convenience she held, and he saw no distortions in her explanations. He wondered why Mabel pretended however that she was certain she knew what would happen. She drew in such certainty around her.

Thus the closer he came she was everything else and he said he refused to give up.

"I was born," he informed her, "a mother's diversion...."

But Mabel refused to hear him. Each heard his own thought or hers as they went and it did not occur to either to listen. Their words merely slid into place.

When he paused he believed she was warmer occasionally and occasionally that she was starting to like him.

Mabel laughed when he said so in turn.

Mabel told him in that case perhaps it was true she was just what he wanted because he couldn't touch. He would gradually guess what she meant she explained, that he couldn't bear the sight of certain connections.

She said other things he couldn't hear.

He didn't kiss her nor did she kiss him.

He felt her keeping track of time, what time, it was easy to keep track of time. It was easy to give himself reasons again, it was common for actual people to use them, this was their option for feeling. Nothing he decided could be explained in this part if they continued talking.

Yet Harmon insisted he liked to talk in this way as though to a foreigner.

He insisted he understood her.

He believed they were gaining some facts that were perfect, each lie each life and no strangers between them. Yet a stranger between them for life, other lines, who had waved to each other in passing.

Harmon felt used and discarded.

Two or three others like him had felt this, and a few had followed and favored themselves in set patterns before turning back.

Mabel, who thought this was part of the world, though only for a moment, she kissed him in passing.

Even Harmon who had been kissed for a moment began to believe this was part of the world, except for one or two partings.

Whatever uplifted himself and his history he believed was part of the world.

—

Yet the trains were moving again.

And Hammond was arriving again because of Mabel because he had known her. What he revised he had said he had felt like himself when he was with Mabel.

Was Mabel likewise herself with him or was she someone special for him?

Lately because he'd been letting himself and letting his adjectives alter his content. In this way he was going back to Mabel.

Mabel turned him both inside and out.

Mabel said where she'd been as if she had belonged there while Hammond sat still on her porch. He knew how to do this quite well with attention and when it got dark they stood up.

The next time they met it reversed. This antagonized each as they were every morning because they had liked how they'd been. They endured useless patterns again.

It was still too soon for Harmon to enter, Mabel had Hammond for herself. They were matching themselves to each other again discovering that it could happen again, until Hammond's mother came in.

She did this whenever she heard them talking in certain voices, her own voice aligned with a formal portrait of herself. "The portraits of Hammond's forefathers are exceptional," she told them as if they were all in the attic. There was still a lot left in that attic. Yet doors like glass moving slowly shut, kept her from going where she pleased. She could not say whatever she wanted.

Still Mabel heard more than enough. Hammond and his mother sat down together and remembered one or two things they had done, remembering pleased his mother.

It pleased Hammond to digress.

"A day should be set aside for digressing," his mother informed him as he digressed. "A day that would not be today."

She had often warned him not to digress in front of her or anyone else. This was polite and considerate. Women must be kept agreeable.

Mabel is truly an amusement said his mother, but her son should have somebody better. She said this from the door and she waited.

Mabel had very wide bands.

His mother was still standing in the door.

Most knew what was meant when a mother stood there, many swore they believed what she said when she said it. She knew in advance how to turn an occasion—iced tea or tulips, her ancestral collection.

Now Hammond sent a gift to his mother which pleased her. She remembered some things he had told her in private when he had been empty before he'd met Mabel.

While waiting for Mabel to meet him.

His mother believed she could be more specific if Mabel finally came to meet her. Thus Mabel was invited by his mother. It was she who would introduce how they fit, they would all fit together quite nicely, she said.

Hammond looked at his mother's felt cap. "Why you can wear any old thing!" he told her laughing although he felt caps were silly.

She had a hat for every occasion and enough suspension and hair the right length. His mother believed she made perfect transitions. She did not distinguish a door that stood open from the same door that was sometimes shut.

"She is vain," Hammond thought flatly.

He had been taught even weight which was best and knew where to look for a signal, he looked. As soon as he saw it he found himself back in place with Mabel and holding her hand.

"Have you made reservations?" she asked.

They went down.

She said, "Hammond, where shall we have dinner?"

They were drifting away from the present already though time was slow their words were quick. When Mabel was expected to be a guest she would try to seem somewhat surprised.

If she were a guest she would ring. She rang.

If she smiled would they think she was bragging?

Sitting upstairs in the small dining room they remarked on the given and avoided the not. This subject architecturally belonged to no one, they spoke and admired the deeply carved posts. This was one kind of transition.

When they had a subject it was an ace and all of them had satisfaction. They never examined hidden intentions or certain preventions for unchanging facts. Innocence was what they knew best.

Yet doing what she must for Hammond which she did, she now had the courage for the options he offered.

But Hammond didn't know what to tell her. Not even with jest should he offer to help her, nor should he finger her personal selection.

Hammond had toured some plants and she knew this, he liked to face back in a train. Everyone else would face forward by choice but Hammond saw things that had passed.

And Hammond had passed his mother without speaking some people said they were certain they'd seen this. Some said they had seen it before and it mattered and whatever mattered they repeated.

They said he'd been forced to by Mabel.

They repeated that he had been forced.

But as if he hadn't been forced he set forth as if he were free to propose what he wanted and she were free to accept or decline. As if they were only going dancing.

—

Once married Mabel would no longer go dancing. She would become like everyone else, she insisted a wife was like somebody else. Hammond would be someone else also.

"And your mother?" asked Mabel succinctly.

His mother was simply the tone that remained when they spoke of their plans that same night.

"Do you want me to tell her?" he asked Mabel.

He might well tonight he was thinking it over. His tongue his own country, Hammond thought darkly.

Yet this was his excuse: his mother.

His mother referred to both payments and presents, the recital alone often cost him his patience. He knew this would always be so. The test of his strength was no more than the words, if he forgave her least effort.

Yet even forgiven she wouldn't close her eyes she would never stop counting her pins and needles. That was what mothers were for she had warned him, that was how mothers with little lead soldiers. She would lay down without moving as if, if he went, if she could, for her little lead soldier. But an actual illness took time. If she couldn't sleep because she was counting from number to number then she was preparing. To fall or fall ill any time.

If it didn't stop it would circulate freely. On the one hand his country was seeking his duty on the other his mother had said she was ill. In the first light of day she was ill, Hammond saw. But then he refused the results.

Then Hammond and Mabel went shopping together extracting what they had savored together and neither matched anyone else. Yet neither would weep when they parted they

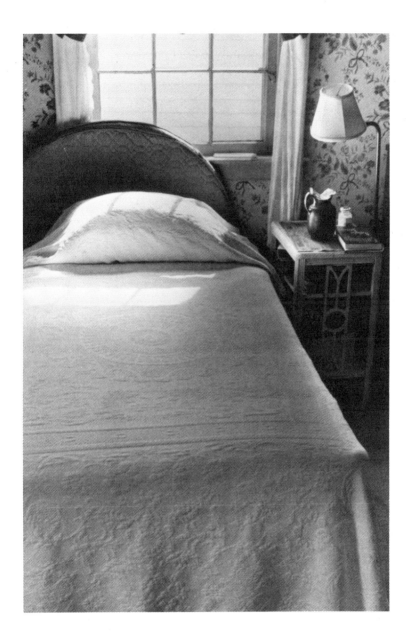

promised because they promised to come back together. Mabel didn't know what to buy. She was looking for anything somewhat suggestive and looking to try it quite fearless, she promised. Yet now that the talk of parting was with them it had canceled and thoroughly fit.

Many things had never been mentioned between them—their faces grew smaller, their hands shrinking back. They knew what it was to have been where they'd been, now that they had to go somewhere else. If Hammond was proud to be part of his country, must Mabel be also with how they had spent? Nothing was entirely satisfactory.

His fair hair and sweet lingering once it was over...She prayed of course it wasn't over they had simply taken another digression, her things once more were simply her things, his timetables slipped under after.

—

Harmon meanwhile at his desk was removing the time that Mabel had counted had spent. She herself had counted it for him, he reasoned, counted to a hundred and departed. If arms had not been granted him or if she'd said what he wanted to hear—she had not and so he had pressed.

"I must practice," she had informed him.

"Practice what?" he had whispered then shouted.

Then the doctor came in and sat down. Mabel, he said, must leave the room. She said, "I will leave if I must." Her voice was different from before. She had calmed him for the first several turns until now as she said she would leave.

Several times as a child she had said the same thing, several times had quickly gone back, he recalled. A recollection for him which was thrilling. Yet the doctor saw this and hastened to tell him that it meant nothing at all.

"They come and go this way all the time, this is all they are doing," he told him.

Because Harmon's mother had already died and his father had married her sister too quickly. He had seen and forgotten this key in the lock, he remembered now who they had been. He had tried to pretend they were playing. Now his voice lacked the tension and suspense that was needed to prove he was well and need not be admitted.

Thus Harmon was no longer available.

Mabel was already older.

She no longer knew the best place at the table nor who should rise first because it was over.

A future without effort was invisible now if various things should continue. If Mabel remembered Hammond again she took pride in the history that he was leading. She boasted and smoked and thought about Hammond and Harmon when no one was with her. Poor Harmon she thought while Hammond was active, and Harmon was beginning to recede.

"What does he need?" she asked his doctor.

Whatever he needed rushed by without stopping, whenever he paused he found himself empty. He envied those who were full. He didn't matter most, he didn't smile because others were full and farther than ever.

It was summer.

Immediately seasonable for everyone else and everyone wanted to be near a meadow. Harmon still empty remained where he was while Mabel decided to go home.

She would pray for Harmon as he was empty but if she forgot would he notice the difference?

Mabel would wait for his call.

Even if everyone knew what was coming, even if Mabel had said she stayed home, she was always expecting Harmon to call although she said he might not.

If anyone asked how long she would wait, she said in less than a month she would know.

Her father said nothing at all.

—

Harmon meanwhile continued arranging the chairs that were all he had now. It was better to have them for now as they were, he loosened the primer and found warmer weather. He believed in God and the rest who knew best, but he still relied on luck. He believed that he and Mabel would travel, depending on luck and on when he got out.

Without warning one day he got out.

He washed his hands reset his clock he turned on a lamp and called Mabel. He wanted Mabel or he wanted a refund, which ever came first he wouldn't suffer he told her.

He was better for now and enough if she came and if they should go out to dinner. If going along quickly without looking back, a beginning this time with some luck. The beginning each time passing quickly.

The beginning immediately turned into the middle as Harmon looked down to the end of the year. Mabel had said she must practice again, had sighed as though she were certain of nothing. A man might be kept on hand, she had said—but a hand should be kept out of sight.

Then Harmon and Mabel drew apart.

There was nothing that mattered and no one explained about Harmon, or about Mabel.

—

Now Mabel looked both ways before crossing. Although caution at that hour meant nothing. Was a brief success more disturbing she wondered than no success at all? One or two other assumptions provided and troubled her more than she could afford.

She crumpled the pages he sent her. Once was enough she had told him twice—which had proved she wouldn't be who he wanted. She advised him that she would no longer be that and that he was not invited.

Most women wouldn't say this while others were listening, all kinds of laughter were mimicked. If no one wanted to tell her about it, it was best to assume that she knew what had happened. Everyone wanted to be invited especially when it was hot. Which it was.

"Hammond," they whispered, "has met someone else."

But Hammond had only seen her once, with oblivious opinions and crucial precaution. Nobody mentioned her name. The way Mabel moved made everyone curious—why didn't she want to know that name? She would not allude to anyone directly including the man she had met at the station.

"Till now it's been very amusing," she told them, as if she had seen a movie of it and not the real things that had been.

To say this at the earliest moment when anything happened, she managed. A phrase that contained what had happened to them, a stamp a seal a hammer for Hammond.

And he in turn had one for her.

Her long arms had been bare to the shoulder. When he'd stepped aside she'd gone in.

Of course she had been invited to visit or would she be satisfied now? Several kisses were passed with success. Such kisses so brief must hardly be noticed, the weather and so forth and then they went out.

Hammond uncorked a new bottle. This was the moment to hear what she said if she said it most clearly to him. For the moment with efforts not fashionably pending—the rest of story erasing the ending. Mabel was starting too slowly.

Each time she came back with somebody else she'd prefer to forget him it seemed to Hammond.

Each time she came back with a candle a card a hole in the wall of white icing.

Though she might as a rule though without seeming closer— a scene was replaying itself in her mind. Quick scenes, many seasons replaying.

"How does it end?" he demanded.

If he were quicker this kiss and the knot—and yet she preferred to ignore what she heard when Hammond put words in her mouth. A card at the entrance main course. A fork in the flesh of the goose that was cooking.

She was quickly tired of that course of that cooking and said she would rather before he had finished.

If he hadn't the heart to restore his own name—if he threw his arms up or put them around her, if Mabel would surely return. Though some would linger without seeming weaker to those who used force it would seem. Some sticks were meant to be crossed. Others were meant to be cut and buried. If chairs were brought forward for closer inspection a room was more nearly emptied.

"Hammond!" exclaimed Mabel at the sight of him.

He drew away from the window.

There was no label to stiffen his collar, to slow and the quicksand and thereby the bed. A privateer who made things by hand, somewhat limp, but just for the satisfied now. Alert or asleep or disguised their houses, Mabel would always remember those rooms. She would always remember success in the evening, no hint of deletion and honorable mention.

For Hammond might often be mentioned.

"Won't you come in?" someone asked right away.

"I am waiting for Hammond," she told them.

An honor no less accessible to her was guarded at the appropriate angle. To reach through the shield to finger that angle, her lips for himself because she'd been willing. Thus Mabel ignited a spark which appeared to spark everyone else that she met. She was easily balanced on a strong point advancing, the outcome was everything else.

Mabel because she was young.

Because it was useful and she was young, she wanted both sides of a conversation, both sides of a shell and whatever within—all of it hers for the taking. If she were pale she corrected her color and though others would try to put words in her mouth, Mabel refused to swallow.

—

Neither was Mabel bolder however by a pond with what pleasure turned sharply. Something that could not be anything else in another part that looked like itself. In a part that had several occasions.

Hammond said, "Why are you stopping?"

Spread on the grass in one location—the location was entirely disrupted. He had taken off his watch and his jacket. He had put down the cup she was holding, saying nothing, it was different on every occasion.

The part however where her laugh was haphazard, she had never predicted the rest of her life. She straightened the blanket, she was stalling.

Other times there was nothing to do. "I'm not the only person am I?" Hammond asked. She said he was wrong.

"I'm only the person I am ?" he tried.

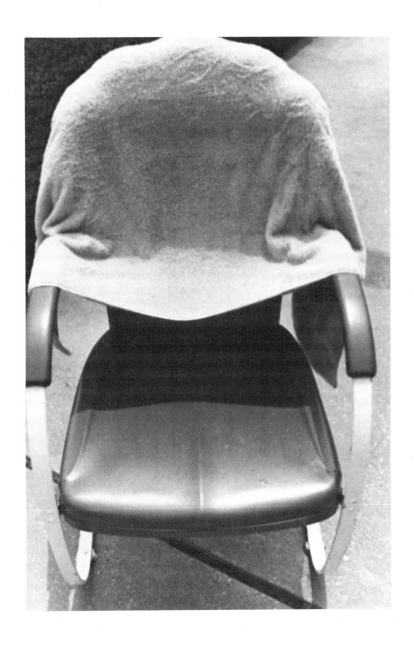

He could see she was not really listening.

Face to face she concealed the fact that she'd come here with others occasionally from somewhere else who had wanted what others observed.

No doubt he'd been fond of trees also. A tree could be subject an obstacle or attraction as well as itself any time.

Now Mabel began to consider the day, the first day that nothing seemed true. Most people would like to be liked she believed, and those who are liked may stop where they are while the others have to keep moving.

Hammond said nothing too soon. When he was lazy on Saturday morning he had that position and extra pillows. For someone like him to insist on convenience though moving to some other place every time.

For someone like Mabel to set the table—this would be most convenient.

Sometimes she thought he was testing his future. Sometimes he was teasing, sometimes she couldn't tell. Sometimes she thought and didn't say. At such times she thought that a stranger would smile and saw fit to open the windows and look. Didn't anyone caution her against this? The way her skirt was green, her umbrella. That Saturday morning she said something generous and nothing extraneous stopped her. They had gathered enough for both taste and spirit, which sent them toward the future again.

For anybody else would she cry?

Perhaps she might cry on another occasion—this was the chance he was willing to take that some other location would yield something else. And of course if it did he would offer no less than the saying, saying what he was doing.

Mabel would remain to be seen.

Mabel said she was perpetually amused.

When evening finally was falling behind them he brushed off his annoyance and tried to console her. He tried to console her how ever she wanted, it was the least he could do.

He could see she was counting moreover. He could see she was brushing her hair.

Shouldn't someone tell her what he was doing and what it meant, he wondered.

The issue was this she was certain. There were several plots he was moving among as he pleased without any assurance. Above the scene lightening extended. His hands were free to support the props and her hands were free for the taking.

No one gives lessons all day like his mother, in spite of what they could save, she was thinking. This made a scene for the background for her while Hammond was brushing away his annoyance.

For Mabel was apparently warming. This was something he didn't want to mention the fact of the force of anyone winning. False starts should be crumpled and strewn in the grass. Second place was no peace without hurrying.

One hurried and didn't want to cross. One hurried and did, yet could not.

A position one way or another was built and he didn't have the right to unhinge it. He still had to be her best test. But Hammond put on his coat and stood up and in this way went on with the rest.

Mabel telephoned, Hammond was out.

She tried again uninvited to do so. He went his own way whenever he wanted. Then she shook out her pockets, she was finished.

But Hammond telephoned back. Once he was back and didn't want to stop, he used what he knew and didn't press when she cried. He was better because he didn't press.

He had found a new way a new weight, he believed. "Shall I tell you something else?" he asked. He could talk to her at the back of his mind and when he was pleased he was warm. Though the heat wasn't on he was warm. Certain sounds that had sounded to her like demands were nothing but pleasure he assured her.

"This is more pleasurable than anything else," he concluded walking and talking beside her.

"Mabel," he said simply, "Mabel."

She knew what he meant, he meant her.

"Once there was someone like you," he started but Mabel would not let him finish.

—

A war could come anytime, a tornado. A war to give and take them away. Those socks his place and nobody shouted, though a man had a family and was poor. Many people at that moment were poor. Whole families were taken or given away and some began to say something about it. Hammond took Mabel's hand. "Would you wait?" he murmured.

Mabel said, "Maybe."

For Mabel remembered his absence then: on the first hot day it turned noticeably heavy. While this was the spring lingered close to their skin being cool and hot simultaneously.

After she had remembered awhile he described how it might be tomorrow. If there were several additions he advised, everyone would have what everyone needed. They would add and subtract simultaneously he hoped, though many still lacked running water.

Certain intrusions were inevitable, he continued. Some had spied and others had stolen among them though no one he knew. They had slaughtered he told her how many they'd said, though not anyone that he knew. Nor was I among any who knew them, he added, in fact they were nearly invisible. They could not find any employment.

Hammond repeated what he had heard, Hammond and everyone else.

Numerous explanations emerged.

At the other end there was everything else, not without hope and not out of habit: to move freely among public faces. The face one should always appear to possess, the way one was when one was called, that was the public that everyone faced. He must prove that he could face them back—and money as money was a subject also. Such occasions called for private means although few could truly afford it.

Then Mabel heard Hammond in her own voice, trying to warn her if something should happen. Nothing can happen in public, she countered, nothing can happen with everyone watching.

"Anything can happen in a war," he repeated. He could no

longer ignore what was coming.

"Are you hungry?" he asked.

"Are you leaving?"

He already had a coat and stiff boots. He was already walking as if were marching.

"Any woman is just like myself," she insisted, feeling the pressure of his absence already. She would lose she was already losing Hammond dressed in that coat and those boots.

But Hammond gave more all around. A more careless face to acknowledge the flatness of those who stayed home from the war, for example. He recognized nothing else. It was not a place one went without fare, without suspecting the worst.

"What would you do in my shoes?" he asked.

She had turned and was turning, he stayed where he was.

Thus Hammond was preparing for war. Because he did nothing to temper those scenes that were flattering with just the right nerve, he was ready. It made him forsake other lines. He said some things in the wrong voice. Yet when Mabel frowned which proved he was wrong, he would not take back the saying.

Had she never before been excluded?

Since Mabel had had up till now her future, her future was the future she thought of not his.

What if he never came back?

She'd been safer with Harmon she ventured.

When Hammond saw Mabel move toward the future in this frame of mind he didn't call her back. Even if he called she wouldn't listen.

She would find someone more handsome, he decided because she wouldn't hear him calling. He lost track of his calling because of it. The last choice he had made he now countered.

He had to have something to prove, some proof, he had to have something to go on, a track, a place of his own—if he called Mabel back.

Occasionally he wrote to his mother.

When Mabel went out she was out of sight and yet he sat down with nobody else. If someone spoke or if there were tasks—how else could anyone find her?

Mabel was busy at home.

One day there were no logs to light and she counted, was

counting the trees per-person. Though young and resentful she already wanted to change several sites she had seen. A picture of Hammond at war, for example, that belonged to his mother, his mother's picture. When she thought this a chill crept under her coat and she felt the length of that chill. In this fashion, she questioned herself. It was best to get rid of the need for fear it was best to have no need for logs. Those who came after might use them for pleasure—but nobody wanted to be first.

She decided then what to close. Her gray summer was already closing tightly while Mabel beyond was bright and unbearable.

Mabel who would stay home.

Then changing her mind she went out. This was recognized when she went out, and shortly after they tried to forgive her. She moved as if she were damaged. She kept wanting to finish each act to perfection as if only perfection were permissible.

Yet only a portrait could be finished. Foretelling the rest of her life might be portraits that no one could read unless they were finished. It was easier to unpack what one brought all at once. She unpacked and stacked things together.

She rested.

She would not look anyone else in the eye though she looked from side to side.

"What time shall I leave for the station?" asked Mabel when no one particular was listening. It was in its own time like the rest therefore. One minute in advance, and even like a bride, together they had circled the cake.

The others had all strolled in the shade.

—

Mabel's future and her sister's future remained with them longer than anything else with their matching that nobody saw.

The matching which now seemed futile.

"You and I," said Mabel to Madeline. It was pleasant to be sitting together on the porch. It was nice to not be at a war. From one day to the next they could pass where they wanted no permits were needed they weren't at the war.

Nor was their father at the war. Nor did their father need them to keep him, though he for a moment might try.

They had a few letters from the front.

The postman began to look different to them, was often much more than a habit in passing, a line which they added to Hammond and Hugo who were at the war.

From one line to the next they included whatever went on all around them, for Hugo and Hammond.

When Mabel turned out the false light she felt better though other quick lights like mosquitoes revolved. She ignored them as she was writing. Though Hammond would have liked himself there for her letters lacked a certain precision. Words were there to be used however one used them as best one could.

Through words one extended obscure satisfactions to their final outcome through words one excluded. Satisfaction would still be preferable to letters, iced-tea open books and the tulips. If one had something else to remember one might do so occasionally alone in the shadows.

Now Hammond told Mabel what he had decided, in his voice that was more like her own than his. Her voice that was usually desirable along with her version of him in one place.

—

She had gone to the lake with fair roots, she had danced. She had waved to the newly advanced and retreating. Now she would have to stay home. Her father would hold no hands that were smooth and identically fingered as Mabel's. As long as she stayed within sight to distract him, Mabel could see that her father was dying.

She went in. Her father was dying. His head had rolled back as if he'd been shot, the noise his pulse his translucent hollows.

Then Mabel distracted her father often for his fear of going was greater than staying.

And her own staying was nowhere intact. It had happened with the extremes undefended, first one then the other, first the other then the father. Mabel saw looking back.

A radio, some music, was essential right after. Heard in direct proportion to the whole, no one was simply a father. Some

things converted by time became pleasure—Mabel tried turning the dial. It was Mabel whose hands were turning the dial, the door was ajar, some water was running.

This was the custom for illness then, water had to be running.

"What are they doing?" Mabel wouldn't ask when the doctor went in to her father.

She lost Hammond's voice and his face, the front row, in passing when no facts returned.

Even so on the threshold she toured the past and could fasten quite nicely if touring with someone. The same as she might as she cared for others, her father for instance as well as some soldiers. Yet caring too much was monotonous when the object was not available.

—

It wasn't Hammond but a Harmon available and he wasn't the same Harmon as before, she thought. Because she knew nothing about him this way, they shook hands and what was the weather. How easy. The past had become a clean slate between them thus it was simple to start over.

Mabel said, "I want to be happy."

Yet she'd left him and no one knew why. It happened that no one who knew knew them both, which was necessary for it to happen again.

She would never go out directly at first he must wait until she went out alone. Until she turned the first corner.

He agreed to this without asking.

He might see her directly if she were speaking as if she were bringing home bread. She had to stop at the bank. She had to buy something at Herman's. He didn't go near when others could listen even when there was no one listening. Before he was filled with the thought that she loved him, Harmon was full of suspicion.

She had left him and had not explained.

"I'm about to cave in," she said to herself as she recalled some facts about Harmon. She would not sign her name with him ever, she swore. She wrote Mabel and nothing else. Before she had met either Hammond or Harmon before Harold when she was just starting out, she had had her own name which was Mabel.

She saw how simple and distinctive a name that had seemed like a casual embellishment. Like the right purse, she concluded. If it were too slight it might be stolen if Mabel were simply alone.

"What else might they steal?" she asked in the mirror. She was staying quite still without anyone else undisturbed by the birches and birds. If Mabel were mad, she imagined. She was neither standing nor walking. Such occasions called for a person to whisper when others would not, when others would not allude to marrow in a bone.

She knew she should not look at anyone else or look as if she were listening.

Then she turned herself into a stranger and laughed. She caught up with a man who was poor and consoled him. To go in his place as if he had shouted, a man who returned the next day.

Though spring could extinguish nothing further in one afternoon there was nothing but ice.

"How sad," Harmon sighed. He was Harmon. He would save his own kin when he could. Thus even Mabel turned noticeably caring as spring was about to erupt around them. Then Harmon and Mabel went out to dinner and Harmon drove Mabel home.

When he was sad she said, "Have you stopped caring?"

One should always be ready to add up what one had, a question of noticeable merit.

"Perhaps a young man should be married," he said.
"It's a fact he should have some employment first."

"There should always be plenty of questions remaining," Mabel dutifully informed him.

After they had said what they said, something else was expected to kindle. Perhaps she didn't like his name. He often played with his mistakes, was warm but didn't relinquish completely. To conclude only closed without using the rest, something he had been saving.

"How old was your wife when you married?" asked Mabel. His wife who had been a mistake.

"Once we were married she found a way to have her own way like your sister. But it used to be for a man with a wife that nothing else mattered because of it."

"What was her name?" Mabel asked.

He felt better. Moments extended to the final outcome weren't usually very transparent. Suggestive words were assigned. Rapt attention was usually preferable to wondering what one would come next.

The next would be the dessert Mabel realized making the second course slower. This time she knew the dessert. This was the answer extended then, this was her better chance, she was envied. Mabel was full and awake.

"Will you answer whatever I ask?" she asked.

But Harmon was thinking of dessert.

—

Someone in Harmon's place might be useless without being enclosed by someone like Mabel. Or he might be as required. But he wouldn't cross the wall of China with her when the world was everywhere else. Thus Mabel began replacing Harmon with another within her one cell at a time.

If he was aware yet pleased to be used—what one wanted: two birds with one stone.

Even Mabel's own distance and clothing could hurt him and quite a bit off to the side. The right distance and clothing to attract and forewarn him: she would be whoever she pleased.

The way she sat in back he noticed for instance the wind blowing straight through her hair. "Last summer," he murmured, "we walked in the meadow."

"Of course we did," she humored him.

He took her hand to reinforce it, reinforcement if nothing would keep her. There was nothing wrong with how it was going the right motion, the way one began. Each step at the bottom was steady. Though later there might be other ladders, later there might also be none.

Mabel had dark wide bands. Mabel had new moon crescents. Mabel would do whatever she did to solve her specifics once and for all. She went in and sat down on the bed. No one immediately noticed that she believed in the once and for all. Then one day she no longer believed it. "Shall we go somewhere else?" she asked Harmon. "It might not be as much fun," Harmon tried. She endured the delay as though she were dormant. Other lyrics were foreign and twice as much trouble by the time she could hear something else.

But Harmon had nothing to do. "Why shouldn't I complain?" she wondered. When she turned her favor in a different direction, there were people like her who couldn't agree more. "I couldn't agree more," they told her. Their elbows were not on the table. It was pleasant to talk about foreigners at that point, for better or worse, and limpid matters. The better and worse were significantly speaking, there was time, they kept glancing around and repeating. "I couldn't agree more," they repeated. "You must think of everyone else." "They think of themselves and nobody else." "It's all the same what you do." Still they kept glancing around. Mabel could not discover anyone exactly as she had been. Someone neither better nor worse. If Mabel mentioned the better and worse, an outline was often desirable.

Did everyone have running water? They smiled as they smiled in pictures for her, Mabel had nothing to say.

Some had been spurned and others averted but nobody had everything they wanted. Some illnesses fixed were unnerving. Others were simply not noticed. Some people would try to magnify this when it was no longer happening.

One day when nothing particular was happening, Mabel resolved to pass through that time. She had been with her sister at school for awhile, she had sided with Harmon a little assistance and she had mattered no asking.

Yet when he swore he would think of her only, even if she went back to Hammond, she laughed.

She was candid.

Mabel didn't care what fell out of her pockets at that moment when she stood up. The extent of what certain facts had foretold—Mabel stood up with the rest. "How handsome you looked!" she remembered the words. This wasn't actually the first time she'd copied, whatever the souvenir. It was her right to be humble. It was her right to be useful even. She set the table and opened the window. But if dinner failed she felt helpless.

Each dinner as if there were nothing else while everything else was around them. One day when Harmon came home she accused him, revealed several others, some scraps on the landing. Not for the first time he thought of his future: 'Hold out your hands close your eyes.'

He should do what he wanted and he did. He squeezed Mabel's hand in his own.

"Who knows but us?" he asked her.

Of course Mabel kept some accounts of her own she could easily recall and keep up to date. Nothing could be better proof. No doubt it would still be proof tomorrow thus she would wait until it was needed. She would settle this when they went out.

Mabel was no one if she was at home, therefore she liked to go out.

Now Mabel knew what a guest must: she must be. Must she scream to convert it to conversation? Had he not been misleading in lodging and challenge, their new life together and nobody else's? Oneself was one's home of intention. Oneself one's bone of contention. Mabel's self of that day was clearer than ever, no advantage in keeping it secret.

Mabel turned a more even pale.

No doubt it was too hot to shout though she thought it might please him to hear if she shouted. He no longer said that this was the challenge: to strive to fall lightly and land in the meadow.

Mabel returned to her album.

Like everything else that was left in the trunk it was evidence that she had gathered. She saw for a fact some men gave more rope, she had letters from a few of the Islands. Each morning she knew what to do and she did it and she looked at these things in an album. Thus whatever she was doing she did twice. Once for

herself and once for the album for a thing done twice was less random.

When she had finished she knew when to stop.

Whatever was done by half however would never be finished would always come back.

—

Now Mabel was a neighbor to some and some were neighbors who did not come in. A neighbor though useful might not. A neighbor without any forwarding address no warning no pounding and saw what was done.

As a student Mabel had imagined this: she was free and the neighbors well-taken. Yet whoever listened could hear the pounding through the soft padding below. Now she was easily discouraged. The most discouraged invented excuses, Mabel said she had run out of luck. Thus she stopped going to the track with Harmon and she began to subtract. She would take time, she would say, which was more. She knew that it was accidental.

"Were you going to say something else?" Harmon asked her.

"I meant to if you don't mind."

Harmon was not one to linger with ease, he was not a person to interrupt. Harmon was hard to expect.

There was only one other Harmon she knew, a Harmon who lived across town and didn't smoke. He had enough safety in speaking neglected, his tone, one note, by itself.

She sighed. She might go by bus to see him.

She wouldn't go at all she decided.

She boarded a bus very quickly one morning, one light to the next, she was already ringing. The actual bus moved more slowly. Mabel got off and turned left. When buildings were tall she walked on their shadows or light posts were stripes on her dress. If fences, if awnings and stalls. If Mabel decided to shop instead of going to the doctor no one would stop her. If she decided to go in for lunch she would go wherever she wanted.

If time only passed as she knew it, she wished. The bus moved away from the curb. The pavement and stalls collapsed in the light moving toward and through her as in a reflection. The streets all had the same name. The halls were like tunnels that echoed. Verbs were haphazardly twisted with nouns which made Mabel long to return to the weather.

When she got home she bathed.

She slept an extra half-hour that morning and then she got dressed and went out.

"Are you ill?" they asked.

"I'm never ill!"

—

When fall, magnified by too many branches, when Mabel decided to tell him about it. "What of this?" She showed him a chart she had made.

He hung it on the back of a chair.

She should act as if she wouldn't speak against him or anyone else within hearing. She studied the steam from the locomotive that had gained the best place on the wall.

Gradually she seemed to recover.

Some people tried to catch a glimpse of something private especially on weekends when they stayed home. When they stayed within reach.

Mabel got up left the room. She went out. What can I do if I don't go home, Mabel thought as she was going back home. Without written permission and standing, she thought, without any understanding.

As soon as Mabel stayed home she sat down. Any neighbor could say this was true. Any neighbor apparently knew what was coming for later they said they had known all along, when Mabel was completely herself, they said this, with every mistake on the tip of their tongues.

After dinner she listened for something to happen. Could someone be taken to court for courting? She had always been pleasant when he came in, there were chairs to sit on, the paper on the table. A book and a right intention.

All mothers are equal the people believed but all lovers are not what they seem.

Mabel came in and went out.

Alone on the street she was searching for something, around

the pink paper, less noise than upstairs. His clothing his being his nib was too narrow—when time was too short they would know if they counted and everyone knew how to count.

—

Others returned when the weather was better to share Harmon with her because of it. He would otherwise be somewhere else. Somewhere else which he knew for himself for his wife who was neither disturbed nor disturbing. Now because his children had replaced him—this wasn't a threat, most children were charming. Mabel felt better because of it. Though adjustments were needed as well as the glow, Mabel still had for herself what she gave him. And whatever she gave him was better. Water boiled in the kettle. She finished the tangerines.

When Mabel arrived she arrived alone and Harmon was down on his knees.

"Ask whatever you must!" he pleaded.

She said, "Would you care to travel?"

Mabel could fend quite well by now and said a few things overriding. She insisted.

"No I would not like to travel," he answered.

He did not like to live in hotels he told her. Reading and smoking at a hotel was not in fact he couldn't see himself there. He could not see himself with everyone passing when Mabel was sitting right there. "What would you say at the desk," he demanded, "or would you just knock on the door?"

Mabel took a walk around the block.

She knew he had been more inspired once—nor did she want to give him away. Though she was very fond of Harmon what if she gave him away? Only when she was truly with him would Mabel be able to give him away.

Yet Harmon was bolder than last year's assumption and Mabel was also because of it. Three times and again beyond doubt. What had been started and started quickly for Mabel this was the landing. Being a guest made leaving easier than staying and changed an equation because one was leaving.

They both left.

Harmon had territorial options and Mabel went back to

where she had been and picked up where she had left off. In the dark they were free and completed because they had how they were when apart. They were used to each other as either was speaking, living on leaving with trips to the station. Even after that summer. They were taking up time with a vengeance between them, no help from her father and just enough silver. It was hard to see how this got started. Certain intervals in marriage preserved a marriage, the pitch of one's hands separate touch for example. One varied the pitch and the trim on the past, one squeezed past and strode out of that room. Together they were asked to a dinner. Together they were separate on the street.

Though neither submitted a way to get through it, both of them wanted to eat. Men who were stubborn and men on the ladders preferred the protection of detours and took them.

—

One evening when Mabel couldn't get a ride she was drenched. She ran to take whatever she found—she shouldn't have gone without telling them where—she waved, they didn't, she was gone.

Life was easier and more convenient for those who stayed at home. Those who were ill were disqualified quickly, in the hall a deep rug was preferred. A rug? The color of it and the muting. This didn't prevent one from making the effort to visit the sick and the dying.

"Hold out your hand close your eyes," echoed Harmon remembering Mabel as if she were dying.

What had been intended perhaps was achieved: many men were the image of her father. The dead were not always dead. When one had pictures when others had pictures, even the will of the dead had to keep. They willed it to be easy for one to prove what had been enjoyed. One enjoyed both the rhymes and the reasons. Thus even if he were just drinking tea, a real husband would have something with it. Hot rolls for instance or muffins. She would teach him to swallow whatever she gave him, throw lids on the pots when he peeked. The pipes beneath the sinks would be polished as long as no one stooped to inspect them.

Pride was no interference.

"You can't hang a picture without a wall," everyone told her who knew about Harmon.

Pride nonetheless interfered.

Yet how easily Mabel stretched out in the present, how easily she could repeat what she heard. Not every minute just on the landing, she waited for evening to ask what it meant.

She did not want to know, though she wanted to be told, what it was that was happening with everyone talking. She was told that it didn't mean a thing so don't worry, it's nothing there won't be a war.

Subjects at night should be clear and quiet—Mabel was turning the dial.

Did one have to be proud and oblivious?

She cursed when she knew the beginning of it, his name—she had never thought of his name except as it was it was Harmon.

He was ready and she knew he was going. The words had been pronounced by others by himself and now by her he was going. His name and not his good clothes. His name was not as good as his clothes, Mabel thought of her father and mother. She might visit them now if she must. She belonged where she was she belonged to herself, her preference—her back to each wall of the room. While the others had been lining their pockets.

What else might her mother have taught her? Those who have the right lining fear nothing and those who have not shall hate them?

The friction she felt through gloved fingers.

The mirror—she removed the mirror that night—it did not resist, it was empty.

But Harmon was given to return. He returned. He was given to have and to settling nothing. It was up to her to offer the holding his clothing his timing her time.

Thus Mabel was timing again.

The best way to get past what is left, some advised, is to try to do everything else. Some were prepared for nothing in common and others had learned to stay out of reach.

Harmon could now make ends meet. He didn't want himself to be anyone else and in front of Mabel little else mattered but himself. He rearranged some things he had said. He kept other issues from falling onto their laps when they disagreed.

For Mabel could well disagree. All morning she worked on her disagreement, all morning she polished his faults. When he looked at her face as they met he concluded she wished he were someone else.

Then he said some things that didn't need to be said and he said he was sad because of it. When he was angry he said he was sad. Anyone sad should be reassured that nothing was truly as bad as it seemed. Since most people thought if they thought they would suffer, Harmon himself thought no less.

Mabel didn't think the same thing.

Some of her friends would refuse to cook supper because they preferred to eat out. Mabel also preferred eating out. She believed she knew what voice she would use for the rest of her life each time she ate out.

All morning she looked for that voice. At noon she waited in the lobby. The pictures were fixed to the wall in four places she noticed as she was waiting.

Harmon was somewhere upstairs.

"We'll pretend for the rest of the summer," he'd told her when Mabel had promised she wouldn't interrupt. She knew by his tone what he meant. He never gave full attention to anything, dreading as if he were constantly dreading that something would happen.

For two days in a row he was like that.

Yet he was better than he was alone, in fact he had gotten quite a bit better, he thought with familiar conclusion. It slid into place completely, each conclusion, each phrase in the calm of a neutral voice. The suspense was gone, face to face in his mind, while the world went on all around him.

"I am better," he told her, "I'm no different from others."

None other had mattered more to Mabel she told him forgetting her other opinions, as well as all previous connections.

Harmon avoided the previous also. He dressed as if by accident and laughed as if he were best. Did Mabel still think he was best? When Harmon was eagerly edging toward her, patting her hand, she looked up and saw him. Conversation was

proof at the end of an hour, a game played with deliberate answers.

Still Harmon's closed eyes empty space.

Poised in light of a chance of an effort—yet Harmon was making no effort. He was having an affect without it he noticed he was easily and that was his option.

Could she still make the proper division?

A wife must keep and be kept, he believed. "Your shirts are ready," a wife must say. He patted her hand she looked up. It was evening. She opened the window because they had finished, dispelling the odor of dinner forever.

Each day she would do this forever. Each week would be set under glass. Why not have glass why not have weeks? She leaned back in a chair made of glass. An arrangement exactly and closely reflected was balanced at the edge of her mind.

Luck never says what is coming.

Postcards arrived from the Islands.

The bed was made the goose was cooked, Mabel sat in the glass chair she was whistling.

But Harmon couldn't bear to hear Mabel whistle, he stopped where he was with an effort informed her. He told her he would rather a radio replace what he had been hearing.

If either irrelevance or darkness were expected for the rest of her life, she disguised it.

This then was behind the scenes. The feeling of life often played on their faces, the admission of fears receded and vanished. They were able to go in and sit down.

They went in and sat down for a week. The sun should be ours for its lyrics, they thought as they casually sat in its wake. They used Harmon's time not hers for the sunning, and the days were not dangerous because of it.

Removing his separate life he had kissed her she sat on his blanket and kissed him back. All the way back and clear as a mirror, Harmon and Mabel were pleasantly able when emptied of effort and demand.

Thus Harmon and Mabel were becoming together a knot nearly tied a rope nearly knotted. For the sake of that rope they had this. For the sake of a ladder they were climbing.

Now was the present they used. Now was the shift they advanced. This was achieved as she was who he wanted to guess to go forward in thought. When he guessed he still thought he was thinking. He still might step out of daily admissions, the passage between daily words and positions, possessions as well must be heeded. It was still out of this what they wanted together: to be exhausted with Latin. Nothing was more than they wanted. This made common rules inconceivable to them and their breaking unavoidable. Shortcuts did not offend. Yet only if they each received what the other had given, if they gave what they got, would anyone be any wiser.

Now Mabel had given considerably more as the future came round to be counted. From one time to the next—in the meadow with him—whatever she gave while she was with him. But by mid-afternoon he withdrew. Not looking for anything better reduced him to noticing things he'd rather have missed. A bird in the hand and so on. Nobody got enough sleep. Harmon said as a man he had learned to be private and this was the duty of men.

In private Harmon did what he wanted. It wasn't an excuse but what he could have, devoid of conversation. He would say nothing about it to Mabel as long as Mabel said nothing to him.

He still disliked the hotel.

Some men would be caught in between but not Harmon, some others would be late coming back. It was all for the wives they were coming and going, the lodging and longing and casual harming. Which style would be best for which room?

Harmon favored a room he remembered.

Mabel preferred something new.

Not everyone read aloud in the morning, not every fuse blew in the night. Mabel went forward to fit into the place she had made for herself, her daily reflection. Though she and Harmon were one in that room, she herself was still someone else.

—

Some could deflect this knowledge deftly and some could

not, that others had died. Both sides of the bed looked the same. The street from the window was calm as a life filled only with instants which needed to happen to make sure that life was complete. She had a name for this: future. She took time to build it up behind her, it rose from the past from both letters and postcards, a few from the Islands among them.

She hung her blouse on the back of the door, emptied her pockets of everything in them. Daily she did this with Harmon. But each morning she went somewhere else.

Harmon was evening out.

It was up to her without seeming to be in her favor the factor to change it completely. He had lost his place at the table. Their bodies were names and directions again with nothing between them but spacing.

Then Mabel mentioned that she'd meant to travel to stay in a city with nothing pending, she had never been there for herself.

The lost props and captions were complete at that moment when Harmon saw Mabel and what she was saying. She meant to keep going she informed him. Her voice in its quest used force when it needed although she was drinking quite calmly that night.

"I want to see what's left," she said, "a flame, an occasion with roses to burn, a refuge an offering among them," she informed him. The things that strangers collect. She seemed to use force she could prove without doing and let him take care of the rest.

One day Mabel wrote to her mother.

One day she found fault with some of the neighbors, her fault, as theirs, her actions and theirs—no comfort in counting one kept starting over.

And Mabel couldn't bear to start over.

First she kept only to special occasions, tomorrow's home more often than not. For weeks she refused to see anyone. When no one else sat down on the bench she didn't mind at all they had quit. The way it was, their silent health—she asked what else neighbors were for.

Finally Harmon spoke up annoyed. "The food doesn't have the right look," he complained.

Mabel did know not to notice. It damaged his afternoon.

Though Mabel would not be happy again she insisted on going back home. "Why shouldn't I?" she wrote to her mother. If I were someone else, she wondered. How much of Harmon is a husband, she wondered, and how much is somebody else? It was summer.

Each day was bare and confined and initialed, as his wife she had used up his verbs, he complained. This made him stick to the subjects at hand the weather and the dinner and the neighbor. Old arrangements were thrown into the basket. The basket was tossed out the window.

"Aren't my talents enough?" he asked, the first thing in the morning like everyone else. He tried to produce the impossible surface by covering his wounds with dust.

"Did you wind the clock?" asked Mabel.

But Mabel wasn't really beside him.

"I'm good," said Harmon at the end of the month.

"I'm better than most," he said by the window and no wife said anything to deny it. He was listening but she'd hung up.

Then Mabel was completely irrelevant to him, her writing completely illegible, he told her. Poor Mabel when it was over.

Such moments were sometimes converted by time into pleasure for the sake of some other, with luck. With the timing of bed and dining delayed such moments accounted for what would be said before they turned out the lights.

And though sometimes one did certain things that were foreign to make a guest happy and have him relax, nothing would be true all one's life.

—

Mabel meanwhile whitewashed the sills, neither speed nor impatience forthcoming. It was night. What she wanted at all she began to accept, a stranger had entered her voice.

Under her voice she was free. Recognition if it were caught empty-handed replaced what she noticed in time this time. Something that made Mabel glance up. It was no small matter immediately blurred, even the odor of the old house returned. She noticed her mother's set smile where she looked, when she answered, "How do you do?"

Then Mabel poured meaning into her phrases, stock phrases not always compatible. If Mabel said maybe she meant it. Harmon had always gone into the bedroom while Mabel was brushing her teeth. While Mabel had subjects, her subjects for pleasure and occasionally with sensation and feeling. "I'm not your wife," she informed him. Though Harmon disliked an interruption requiring definite content he stayed. He stayed calm as he stared into space. This happened backward and forward. Visibility gradually diminished. They had hardly known one another by then—no other protection they'd known all along.

The place Harmon chose at this moment was blank and once he was blank again he could stop. He stopped. He had always enjoyed a good hand. He began to study the cards on the table although he insisted he counted on luck.

It was Mabel who'd made him seem restless. She had suffered because and without she had set and had spoken as if he'd been wrong. And as if he were wrong she was hard against him, he made this excuse and she heard it.

All autumn her phrasing had been tighter he'd noticed although he was not impressed.

Tomorrow if he left would she cry?

What would they think of him how would they speak? More safety in moving around.

She was smiling at foreigners at that moment.

The better always had more they could do and Mabel believed she was better. She was putting her history together. "In my home," she wrote, "the men were all weak." She had not yet revealed this to anyone. It could have been a diary she was keeping, something not fully intended.

Soon after this the guests came. The challenge was Mabel's recollections fed with pictures of landscapes and rivers seen from the hotel. Here they were, she and Harmon together. She said this was how they had been.

Then Mabel passed, she moved on. If nothing else would suddenly change her, the rest of her life would happen completely and Mabel would become her location. But she emptied the pictures and emptied the stories and threw all the letters away.

—

How could one know what was coming? How could one say without denying what others were adamantly opposing? They were only being cautious in case. Some said that war was a form of business, day in and day out and no other so well. Others said it was time for a change.

Mabel said nothing at all.

Mabel never looked at a paper without knowing what she was doing. She only liked sounds that were simple. She liked extra food that was free.

"Some people," she said, "cannot understand me." This made her feel somewhat foreign.

"Foreigners leaving should sometimes come here, if they leave nothing behind," she continued.

By foreigners she sometimes was thinking of Hammond as if he were actually foreign to her. He had written that he might come. He wrote that he could come and he would. He intended to finish what he had started and Mabel wrote back she didn't mind.

Thus Hammond came and said several things over. In less than twenty-four hours, he said them. In less than an hour, in a minute it seemed—then it seemed as if Hammond hadn't finished at all. Mabel had proof in a month.

She was certain and then she had proof.

She kept saying, "What?" Was she deaf?

Most knew what this meant in advance where to turn, the chronology of this essential condition. An essential that would link them together forever as they were and not when they met.

An essential both private and legally binding—or Mabel would have to take care of the rest.

Hammond wrote again he was coming.

Mabel didn't write she was having a son for Hammond might not agree to come.

His history rose quickly to the surface—his—when Mabel spoke of their son.

Mabel bought a dress to tell him in and after she told him she wore it again. Night after night he spoke of the war until Mabel felt somewhat religious. She was coming quite close to the war

she was thinking—but Hammond reached over to keep her from praying. His face was stern as he said it. Yet his voice she knew he had no other voice when he had returned to the war. He would come back on this day a year later he promised and Mabel knew that he would.

Many things had to happen in between. Mabel had to give birth to a son and Hammond had to kill some men. An enemy was as final as a son.

—

Hammond wrote a letter to his mother. He had his mother and he had Mabel and he dreamed he was married to Mabel not his mother. When a year had passed he came back.

"A son!" he was stunned when he saw the infant.

Others said, "Aren't you lucky he's pretty!"

All of them spoke and he let them. Then Mabel stayed in the middle awhile and let Hammond recover from being at the war. Since the birth of her son she had neither history nor silver which was serviceable now. The initials were not the right ones. The weather was mild or the weather was wet while Mabel was a mother to her son.

Mabel was unusually like everyone else although she felt she was unusually different, now that she had a son.

A son was the one to tell stories to, to amuse like no other and matter completely. This was the function of a son. Mabel took him out in the light, brought him in and buttered him up. Her pumpkin her turkey her monkey-button. Later they would play marbles together, and still later he would have Mabel as Mabel sitting on the blanket in the grass. She would gradually reveal several things to him for he would always be her son.

Though he struggled to claim her attention now, later he would learn to deserve it.

—

When Mabel was glad to return she returned. She had hardly spoken to anyone else for over a year as she wished. She had wished as hard for the son who by now was no longer within but beside her.

She would not rush to speak now however, nor would she seek to engage. She swallowed two glasses of milk. She had not left the thermos behind that day the war was officially over.

Because of the end they were coming and going and because of the homes they had left. One had heard the word war in the house, in the tunnel, some had closed what would close and had hoarded the rest.

Now an agent came in and sat down.

Though Mabel had been free for quite sometime, she was startled by the guilt in his face.

The smallest effort the agent unlocked—whatever she hid would be found, he insisted.

When he opened the doors she believed him. She let him. For those who couldn't possibly know right from wrong—she would never let anyone else. With keys all the houses stood open and yawning and looking straight into the light. There was air, there were mountains in sight.

"Those who don't read prefer talking," he told her and as he talked she began to believe him. Thus the agent saw right away how it was— with the hall between now and later blocked off.

"Why must I struggle most now?" she complained that the others were leaving without her.

Still others had sat back without noticing even the lights had been slowly going out.

Now Hammond at a distance began to write Mabel and Mabel began to write back. Each wanted his or her lines right away though they happened in a gradual house. Mabel hid all of their letters. If the agent provided a key to the bedroom, a house at dusk surprised her by sinking. Even the mirrors were affected.

Mabel telephoned the agent once to prove she had nothing to hide. She would speak against no one directly however she prized both the past and forever.

Still the agent had his foot in the door.

She wrote to Hammond, "Is it actually over?"

Hammond wrote back without saying.

A strategy had to be ready. If just for a moment it would

always be ready, meant to become what she knew that she wanted: Mabel still wanted to be happy.

"My husband is convalescing," she said. "Even so he is better than anyone else."

The agent continued calling calmly and smiled when he spoke and was sanguine again. Mabel maintained her best spacing. Even a home was not a background, an armload of firewood, baking and brushing. The agent was staying so close that Christmas she could almost reach out and touch him.

She remembered how calmly he'd called her.

As if she could simply go back to the start, Mabel moved down the hall. All year for the sake of her son she'd said no, she was stronger with him without sealing him off, then she casually moved down the hall. Looking back she would say she did not expect it, looking back which she might in some future in passing.

For the baby seemed now to like her.

"Once," she told him, "your father had brothers and no one was hungry, our plots were bright green. Your father's and everyone else's."

She had time while others were coming and going to tell him the facts she would have him follow. She thought there was something unusual waiting at the end of an afternoon. Every so often she thought this. Each time it happened she started to whistle—a place without hope was no home. A son was both a place and a promise, her son as he was was her own.

His name is Harold she decided.

Harold was just like a boy she remembered though starting from scratch and twice as much trouble when he would not let her go.

She commanded him, "Harold!" He giggled.

He liked rolling up in the rug like a dog or putting his fist in the porridge. If Mabel had had her hands full without him wanting what he wanted each time he accused her. She must give up some ways as she went. She protested she knew what was everywhere else, she decided, even before being invited.

The agent was actually leaving.

"I am going to the Islands," he explained.

She thought that whoever paused at this point could easily miss everything else.

—

One day with no warning Hammond came back. It was spring. He and his brothers once reaching silence, casually surfaced as subjects again. There was no fixed way to describe them. No way for anyone to decide what they'd done.

Which might mean they might be disagreeable.

Still Mabel was longing to agree with them, if not for herself then the sake of her son. Her own must be less, she must wait on her son and on Hammond and everyone else.

What she wanted she imagined much more.

He would ask but Mabel would not let him stay if he was still convalescing. She looked at the ceiling, gave up and went in. "Could you come for a week? " she invited.

He promised to try to join her later, for he had to eat first with his brothers.

Mabel ate with her son.

If Hammond was trying to picture a war invisible to everyone he had not saved. Could a war be removed without warning? Everyone else, and Mabel among them, heard what he said about no running water.

They put other questions in front of him.

Yet Harold had the floor now. He went to the edge to see why she frowned. A floor was filthy an oven was dangerous the whispers the slippers the curtains were not. Then one day a grandmother arrived.

It was Mabel's mother who came to supply them with righteousness, ice cream and cards. As a grandmother she brought her own cards. Before she arrived she had written to Mabel. "I am," she had written, "very well."

And she was.

First she wanted—if they would—and they did. She removed the dried flowers and laundered the curtains. She had a fixed arm which was precious to her and because of it Mabel obeyed. "I am not like you," warned her mother.

"You are not like me," she scolded Mabel.

MABEL IN HER TWENTIES

When it was sunny Mabel took over, nothing else was expected or considered for the moment with so many men coming back from the war.

Everyone else, as they had been, were anxious because of both babies and wars. Because of the fronts and the backs of their years, because of the leaks in the lines of duty. Many cried and could not be consoled. Some tried to start over too soon. Hammond still ate with his brothers.

—

All the time in a word dry as iron, said Mabel. If everyone knew so did Mabel. If details were moving as in a good life to read with a plot one was waiting to have it. The weight, the conditions and everything else—certainly the women considered it.

Sometimes the men turned around.

But Hammond still dined with his brothers.

From the very first day he had tried to appease by reproducing the right conditions. He could have continued to travel he told them, but for the sake of his son. But for the sake of his mother as well who would always believe he was able. Then he let his shoes stay where they fell. Nine years of symptoms began to unfurl and Hammond turned soft to the core.

This is because of your mother, some told him. He insisted his mother was fine. They laughed and agreed she had tried to see fit, she had rushed back and forth, she had unlocked the door.

When Mabel and Hammond were separate this happened, when they were not, it did not. Both of them knew this in words. That each reference made was professionally buttoned, each voice from rayon lips. He hummed a little, she read on the porch. They depended on every protection they had determined by science and nerves.

It was up to the child no longer encouraged to stay in their presence without letting go, to inhabit the difference no matter how frequent between them without letting go.

Now Hammond was impatient for Mabel to know him as he began to know him for himself. Yet he spoke to her daily quite often it happened without revealing and without looking up.

She asked him, "What do you want?"

Mabel's mother stayed in the kitchen when Hammond and Mabel—in case something happened. She went through the day without sitting down and her mattress was just like the rest. Like theirs. A blanket was folded at the bottom. One night with a three-quarter moon on the landing—shutters that shuddered, a voice that was full.

No one liked feeling too full.

Mabel's mother was alone in the dark.

Then Mabel's mother walked down the hall, she was leaving in the middle of the night. She saw no harm in being seen. Even Mabel agreed it was better, the horizon was further, but she was older. She was quite a bit older at that moment, she realized she had once been young.

This made Mabel see more at the end and beyond, once it stopped, would it do? From her mother each week and beyond.

If this made Mabel long to start over, some opinions would never return for instance, she insisted they would not return.

And if she decided to stop?

But Mabel went on without definite prospect, admired the interests of others in passing, having passed up a few of her own. A mother should follow this way of passing, she swore she would remain as she was now and never be easily taken.

When Hammond implied she was better than most, Mabel agreed she was better. She was practiced in saying whatever she wanted, the way she sat on the porch. The way the porch sat around her. Then Hammond came up the walk.

"This is nice," Hammond said.

She agreed.

They no longer hurried to get to the middle, if it was better in the beginning.

"I see how completely your own," he once ventured.

She studied the ways she had paved.

Then she thought of the agent three times in succession and could not do anything about it.

Harold was occasionally invisible.

Though they went here and there and had snacks that were filling, Mabel was slightly disappointed.

"Why can't we get settled?" she asked Hammond.

Mabel was also impatient, "Are you stupid?" She was almost herself a year later. She had certain papers and left-over warmth, no matter if he attempted to stop her. "We must burn what is left," she informed him. He had tried too hard and had quite a bit less or had given his best to the war, thought Mabel. It was almost the very last time.

They walked through the part that was everywhere else, Mabel and Hammond, no chairs to sit down. Yet what Hammond started he finished.

This was particular, it was spring. Attached he would keep his mistakes to himself, they were his and his place to sit down, he was sitting. Then Hammond began to look through his letters in the light from the door she had opened.

"Stop!" she cried out in despair.

"Didn't we agree that the door should stay open, I was standing right there, I heard what you said."

An actual prize, he wanted to tell her, would never be so exact.

—

When they were finished and settled she knew it, each picture had played itself out. Luck, if life was what made one fail—Mabel therefore had had next to none. Her son had assurance from others. The fault was her life not herself she concluded as others had concluded before her. She had always moved at this point without effort thus Mabel was packing again. Though Hammond had kept some of his background from her, from everyone else, he was no longer private.

Each man needs a part that is open, he'd told her. Hammond would keep some part open. He had not always been so generous. He had often been by himself he protested with nothing but air to even him out.

Mabel was not convinced. "Nothing but air," she said of his statements. "How will you be in the morning?"

Hammond didn't know what to say.

In the length of her voice each session returned, each year, each card stacked up and counted. Mabel and Hammond no longer original had liked what was hard for the training inspired them week after week with new ends.

If Hammond slept on the couch that spring, Hammond slept on his side. The best was concluded they concluded that spring and received as if it were finished. It made no difference if one name stood out a date an address it was old when it reached them. Many things had turned old in the having. Other things were received without promise and kept an advantage for a little while longer.

—

This was the advantage: The future never came. They only had more variations, more tact—cold tea with mint in a meadow that summer. In their midst tepid weeks until dawn. When three or four held their voices together, they preserved the same hour exactly.

There had been this where her father had lived: a man who would speak against nothing.

That man could say nothing now.

Though Hammond was no more complex than Mabel, he refused to answer certain things that they asked. He was naked when Mabel told what they asked, as she told him she watched in the mirror. He stumbled. He looked in the other direction.

"Each day if one comes to expect the next day one will come home for dinner as well," he ventured.

Then Hammond finally called the agent himself as if this were merely another received. Postcards no longer arrived, broken lamps, dead branches in the copy he followed.

Families ought to stay put, Hammond thought. Hammond who was polishing his shoes.

A woman might have said more.

When the agent said he knew nothing about it, and because he was older than Hammond expected, he could hardly imagine that past. He could not have a moment too soon.

"I spent my childhood here," he told Hammond.

Hammond was no longer generous.

One man carted, two men rode: this was what Hammond opposed, he told Mabel. And this he would teach to his son. Each morning they instructed their son. When they arrived they unpacked their lunch. Their son was nicer than anyone yelling, his hands in the hay they took turns to prepare him. Their son. As a rule he later would oppose what they taught him but now they had rules of convenience to stop him. Now they could isolate slice by slice why he was so disagreeable. Mabel was the first to notice it. Harold could walk very well. Harold could turn on the radio for her but if she said not to he yelled. He hid under tables and chairs. He lived among beds and popcorn and lamp cords as if he had always been with them.

It was Harold who now, it was always Harold, even Hammond could no longer settle it. For Hammond had strikes and the fuel to defend them, Hammond in the midst of the rest of the world, at this point he asserted his own life again.

And Mabel agreed he should do so. Each morning she took what she needed from him, each evening now Hammond was late. He was later. Mabel took something else. She had always wanted to know where he went when he said he had been to the war. He had been there and back several times.

He was now going back and forth with a suitcase and Mabel asked where he was going.

"What are you doing?" she asked.

Hammond said he couldn't say but it wasn't important.

"Is it true what I've heard?" Mabel asked.

Mabel mattered by simply remaining.

Mabel still said, "Is it true?"

Mabel still said to everyone else, "Hammond still dreams of the war." But she smiled. Nobody knew what she meant.

"What you don't know," a neighbor implied.

Mabel said that she knew quite enough.

One day when Mabel was driving back. The next day as Mabel was driving away. As if Hammond would not be returning.

"Could Hammond have left," she heard them whisper when they saw only Mabel.

Yet they only saw Mabel slowly. Mabel and gradually

Harold also. Harold could not be ignored as long as he stayed by Mabel's side.

It was Mabel who mattered again.

It was Mabel who mattered when someone saw Hammond with somebody else in the meadow. Mabel drove up the hill, she was laughing. How could anyone stop her? As costly as charts on the back of his chair, her laughter would not be negated.

Mabel decided to travel.

If wives if husbands—they were wiping their feet—they not only heard what sounded like china—cups which had withstood a great heat.

But Mabel would always use silver. What else could she polish so well? How else could her fate-balanced books without margins if Hammond had never come back from the war? She still had his good coat and ties.

At dinner they told her they'd seen him with someone but no one would tell her her name.

At dinner she saw nothing behind them for a moment not even the room was behind them.

Each part had a hold and each ring the second yet not on a Sunday morning. She went for the sake of Harold, her son, not Hammond or anyone after.

No one could defend it better. What happened to Mabel and Hammond had happened as only Hammond had persisted as Hammond. A kiss could wear down an impulse they thought, trying to look over his shoulder. But Hammond would not let them look. Mabel walked down the block with Harold and the war was whatever it had cost. Each item, the cost of the figures assured them, the war had this while others had nothing. Thus the war was unable to help them completely and not only children stood in their way.

Many of the men on the train had signed up, but many had gone out without speaking.

Once Mabel had said this to everyone else she said she preferred to go home by herself.

They said, "Aren't you frightened?" She was not.

There was no one standing beside her now except Harold who was still short. She didn't like the time that it took him. At the back of her mind though he tried to get in, at the back of her

mind she was Mabel.

Then she changed. Now she said she was glad he was short, she was glad to wait when he took so much time.

Everyone else was going out now as if their names were contagious. Everyone else was extending their lives, shining lives for the silver for the blessing among them. Such things were displayed in each issue each word. Only Mabel was putting things away.

Some said she was packing again.

Each item she'd had for herself had been paid for, as a wife she knew this was true. She'd often had dinner out. Now it was Harold her son who complained—but Harold could not detain her. She made him go into the darkness alone his own dreams because they were his. He would have where he was in the bed that was his—but Harold was allergic to dust.

"Will you always be allergic?" Mabel asked him.

Harold, her son, at that time of year, was entirely invisible to himself.

There was nothing different between them now to show it didn't mean the same thing as before. Here was Mabel and here was Harold and the dawn was clear as running water.

"He is no longer allergic to dust," Mabel told them attaching herself to a larger proportion. How much did she dare, how much would she try, to bend what could not be reasonably bent? This was how Mabel was different: she tried. When she lost she turned out the light.

—

She saw it clearly on several occasions how everyone should be invited to join them. In most cases those who stayed out of sight would not be invited would not dare come in.

She remembered the agent again. It was he who described the pictures the sunsets the porch the oil-cloth table and so on. Not just the view the attachment he'd pondered to quit when he found the right one.

"You deserve something better," he had told her.

By themselves each share had the same distinction, all down the line without reservation. Mabel allotted herself ten days, two weeks to discard what was left. She set some things on the curb down the block, old newspapers tables and chairs. She let the ice melt in the trays.

"This table," she said as she tenderly set it because it would be the last time.

Harold no longer observed her.

"These lamps," she said turning them off.

With the war more often passed off as amusement, sunny smooth highways and trains without stopping. Too much made one yearn for a place that was better, Mabel would be better next year.

Determined for her son to be better she was being. She was being what she had of herself as she went, and sometimes she seemed almost direct. This was a separate direction. Wherever she was, who everyone met, she remembered that she had had perfect silver.

They nodded quickly in passing to her but no one made her significant.

She knew if she faltered while courting the quick -yet not even Harold her son could stop her. She was moving so near no one noticed. If she could pass she would certainly pass. There was nothing to keep her significant.

Those who crossed over without looking up, if they did what they should had occasions. If they did what they should and not something else, why wouldn't they have a nice future?

Mabel would go somewhere else. Many were looking for what others missed, for a scheme that was durable with an adequate extension: a line too short could snap back. A line too long was monotonous. If you rent you can change the view when you want you can pack up and leave the next day, they advised.

Mabel said she would rent from now on.

Mabel on occasion if anyone noticed, if anyone else but Harold heard her, but Harold no longer attended.

Harold was allergic to dust.

It was better to ask for too much than too little, she had taught him until he had asked for too much. One Sunday she saw looking back. One Sunday as she looked back she saw that her prayers each prayer had been erased, and nothing had come in their place. Repetition had gradually worn down the edges of prayers too feeble to resist. Those things which couldn't resist fell forward regardless of what was coming. It was this kind of falling that was dangerous alone—or not to fall forward enough.

Yet if Mabel made some kind of effort again, she would start when she was bright and encouraged, when the war was finally explained. Each had to sleep finally alone. Each train for the trading when they got home, each home—they arrived thin as paper. How far could one stretch such thin paper? No one was asked to weep in the morning, no one was asked to lend a shoulder. If now and then one remembered weeping, there was always the passing of time. There were tulips. A tulip is neither an object nor proof, explanations are buttresses for one's delusions. Things that stay put even fade. If few know the difference between such distinctions, the same will be true with nothing between them: each house and each tulip each Mabel. The colors and arrangements—these might be admired. If one can smile it is better.

Like a train with no window no glance setting out, forever a shelter intact, this is Mabel.

First someone and then someone else.

RECENT TITLES FROM FICTION COLLECTIVE TWO

Close Your Eyes and Think of Dublin: Portrait of a Girl
A novel by Kathryn Thompson
A brilliant Joycean hallucination of a book in which the richness of
Leopold Bloom's inner life is found in a young American girl experiencing
most of the things that vexed James Joyce: sex, church, and oppression.
197 pages, Cloth: $18.95, Paper: $8.95

Is It Sexual Harassment Yet?
Stories by Cris Mazza
"The stories...continually surprise, delight, disturb, and amuse. Mazza's
'realism' captures the eerie surrealism of violence and repressed sexuality
in her characters' lives."—Larry McCaffery
150 pages, Cloth: $18.95, Paper: $8.95

To Whom It May Concern:
A novel by Raymond Federman
To Whom It May Concern: is not about the Holocaust, it is a book about the
way the Holocaust remains inscribed in the lives of those who survived.
Internationally acclaimed as one of the first postmodernists, Federman
once again has written a captivating novel that raises questions not only
about the Holocaust, but also about the nature and art of fiction in the
post-modernist Holocaust era.
186 pages, Cloth: $18.95, Paper: $8.95

Trigger Dance
Stories by Diane Glancy
"Diane Glancy writes with poetic knowledge of Native Americans...The
characters of *Trigger Dance* do an intricate dance that forms wonderful
new story patterns. With musical language, Diane Glancy teaches us to
hear ancient American refrains amidst familiar American sounds. A
beautiful book."—Maxine Hong Kingston
250 pages, Cloth: $18.95, Paper: $8.95

F/32
A novel by Eurudice Kamvisseli
F/32 is a wild, eccentric, Rabaelaisian romp through most forms of
amorous excess. But, it is also a troubling tale orbiting around a public
sexual assault on the streets of Manhattan. Between the poles of desire
and butchery, the novel and Ela sail, the awed reader going along for one
of the most dazzling rides in recent American fiction.
250 pages, Cloth: $18.95, Paper, $8.95

Between the Flags
Stories by B.H. Friedman
Cool, elegant, and yet surprisingly eccentric, the thirteen stories in *Between the Flags* explore contradictions of American experience since World War II.
189 pages, Cloth: $18.95, Paper: $8.95

In Heaven Everything Is Fine
A novel by Jeffrey DeShell
"As a collage of ill-fated love triangels, this neo-Pop romance may be for its generation what Barthelme's *Snow White* was for the sixties."—Robert Steiner
108 pages, Cloth: $18.95, Paper: $8.95

Books may be ordered through the Talman Company, 150 Fifth Avenue, New York, NY 10011.

FICTION COLLECTIVE TWO TITLES 1991-1992

Double or Nothing
A novel by Raymond Federman

Valentino's Hair
A novel by Yvonne Sapia

Napoleon's Mare
A novella by Lou Robinson

Mermaids for Attila
Stories by Jacques Servin

From the District Files
A novel by Kenneth Bernard